CLAP

WHEN

YOU

LAND

ELIZABETH ACEVEDO

CLAP WHEN YOU LAND

HARPER TEEN
An Imprint of HarperCollinsPublishers

HarperTeen is an imprint of HarperCollins Publishers.

Clap When You Land
Copyright © 2020 by Elizabeth Acevedo
All rights reserved. Printed in the United States of America.
No part of this book may be used or reproduced in any manner
whatsoever without written permission except in the case of brief
quotations embodied in critical articles and reviews. For information
address HarperCollins Children's Books, a division of HarperCollins
Publishers, 195 Broadway, New York, NY 10007.
www.epicreads.com

Library of Congress Control Number: 2020933571
ISBN 978-0-06-288276-9 (trade bdg.)
ISBN 978-0-06-301670-5 (special edition)

Typography by Carla Weise
20 21 22 23 24 PC/LSCH 10 9 8 7 6 5 4 3 2 1
❖

For my grand love, Rosa Amadi Acevedo,
& my sister, Carid Santos

———

In memory of the lives lost
on American Airlines flight 587

El corazón de la auyama,
sólo lo conoce el cuchillo.

—DOMINICAN PROVERB

CAMINO ✈ YAHAIRA

I know too much of mud.

I know that when a street doesn't have sidewalks
& water rises to flood the tile floors of your home,
learning mud is learning the language of survival.

I know too much of mud.
How Tía will snap at you with a dishrag if you track it inside.
How you need to raise the bed during hurricane season.

How mud will dry   & cling stubbornly to a shoe.
Or a wall. To Vira Lata the dog & your exposed foot.
I know there's mud that splatters as a motoconcho drives past.

Mud that suctions & slurps at the high heels
of the working girls I once went to school with.
Mud that softens,   unravels into a road leading nowhere.

& mud got a mind of its own. Wants to enwrap
your penny loafers, hug up on your uniform skirt.
Press kisses to your knees & make you slip down to meet it.

"Don't let it stain you," Tía's always said.
But can't she see? This place we're from
already has its prints on me.

I spend nights wiping clean the bottoms of my feet,
soiled rag over a bucket, undoing this mark of place.
To be from this barrio *is* to be made of this earth & clay:

dirt-packed, water-backed, third-world smacked:
they say, the soil beneath a country's nail, they say.
I love my home. But it might be a sinkhole

trying to feast   quicksand

mouth pried open; I hunger for stable ground,

                                        somewhere else.

———

This morning, I wake up
at five a.m. Wash my hands & face.
There is a woman with cancer,

a small boulder
swelling her stomach,
& Tía Solana needs my help to tend her.

Since I could toddle,
I would tag after Tía,
even when Mamá was still alive.

Tía & I are easy with each other.
I do not chafe at her rules.
She does not impose unnecessary ones.

We are quiet in the mornings.
She passes me a palm-sized piece of bread;
I prepare the coffee kettle for her.

By the time Don Mateo's rooster crows,
we are locking up the house, Tía's machete tucked into her bag.
The sun streaks pink highlights across the sky.

Vira Lata waits outside our gate.
He is technically the entire neighborhood's pet,
a dog with no name but the title of stray;

ever since he was a pup he's slept outside our door,
& even if I don't think of him as solely mine,
I know he thinks of me as his.

I throw him the heel of bread from the loaf,
& he runs alongside us to the woman with cancer,
whose house door does not have a lock.

Tía knocks anyway before walking in.
I do not furrow my brow or pinch my lips at the stench
of an unwashed body. Tía crooks her head at the woman;

she says I have a softer touch than she does.
I murmur hello; the woman fusses in response;
she is too far gone into her pain to speak,

& since she lives alone, we have no one to ask
how she's been doing. I rub a hand across her
forehead. It is cool, which is a blessing.

She settles down with a deep sigh the minute I touch her.

I bring the bottle of water Tía passes me
up to her lips; she sips with barely there motions.
It is said she was once a most beautiful woman.

I lift the blanket that Tía wrapped
around her the last time we were here
& press gentle fingers to her nightgown-covered abdomen.

Her stomach is hard to my touch.
Tía burns incense in all the corners
of the small house. The woman does not stir.

It is easy in a moment like this
to want to speak over this woman,
to tell Tía there is nothing more we can do,

to say out loud the woman is lucky
that her lungs still draw breath.
But I learned young, you do not speak

of the dying as if they are already dead.
You do not call bad spirits into the room,
& you do not smudge a person's dignity

by pretending they are not
still alive, & right in front of you,
& perhaps about to receive a miracle.

You do not let your words stunt unknown possibilities.

So I do not say that her dying seems inevitable.
Instead, I brush her hair behind her ear
& lay my hands on her belly—chanting

prayers alongside Tía
& hoping that when we leave here
Vira Lata, & not death, is the only thing that follows.

———

Tía is the single love of my life,
the woman I want to one day be,
all raised eyebrows & calloused hands,

a hairy upper lip stretched over a mouth
that has seen death & illness & hurt
but never forgets how to smile or tell a dirty joke.

Because of her, I too have known death,
& illness & life & healing.
& I've watched Tía's every move

until I could read the Morse code
of sweat beads on her forehead.
So, when I say I want to be a doctor,

I know exactly what that means.

This curing is in my blood.
& everyone here knows
the most respected medical schools

are in the United States.
I want to take what I've learned
from Tía's life dedicated to aid & build a life

where I can help others.

There have been many days
when Papi's check comes late,
& we have to count

how many eggs we have left,
or how long the meat will stretch.
I don't want Tía & me to always live this way.

I will make it.
I will make it.
I will make it easier for us both.

———•———

The Day

I am beginning to learn
that life-altering news
is often like a premature birth:

ill-timed, catching someone unaware,
emotionally unprepared
& often where they shouldn't be:

———

I am missing a math test.
Even though Papi will get in a taxi upon arriving,
I skipped my last two periods so I could wait at the airport.

I'll make up the exam tomorrow, I convince myself.
Papi's homecoming, for me, is a national holiday,
& I don't rightly care that he's going to be livid.

(He reminds me once a week he pays too much money
for my fancy schooling for me to miss or fail classes.
But he shouldn't fuss since I'm always on honor roll.)

I also know Papi will be secretly elated.
He loves to be loved. & his favorite girl waiting at the airport
with a sign & a smile—what better homecoming?

It's been nine months since last he was here,
but as is tradition he is on a flight the first weekend in June,
& it feels like Tía & I have been cooking for days!

Seasoning & stewing goat, stirring a big pot of sancocho.
All of Papi's favorites on the dinner table tonight.
This is what I think as I beg Don Mateo for a bola to the airport.

He works in the town right near the airfields,
so I know he's grumbling only because like his rooster
he's ornery & routinized down to every loud crow.

He even grumbles when I kiss his cheek thanks,
although I see him drive off with a smile.
I wait in the terminal, tugging the hem of my uniform skirt,

knowing Papi will be red-faced & sputtering at how short it is.
I search the monitor, but his flight number is blank.
A big crowd of people circle around a giant TV screen.

———————

(Tía has a theory,
that when bad news is coming
the Saints will try to warn you:

will raise the hair
on the back of your neck,
will slip icicles

down your spine,
will tell you *brace brace*
brace yourself, muchacha.

She says, perhaps,
if you hold still enough,
pray hard enough,

the Saints will change fate
in your favor.
Don Mateo's AC was broken

& the hot air left me sweaty,
pulling on my shirt to ventilate my chest.
Without warning   a stillness.

A cold chill saunters through a doorway in my body,
a tremble begins in my hands.
My feet   do not   move.)

———————

An airline employee
& two security guards
approach the crowd

like gutter cats
used to being kicked.
& as soon as the employee

utters the word *accident*
the linoleum opens
        a gnashing jaw,

a bottomless belly,
        I am swallowed
by this shark-toothed truth.

———

Papi was not here in Sosúa the day that I was born.
Instead, Mamá held her sister Tía Solana's hand
when she was dando a luz.

I've always loved that phrase for birthing:

dando a luz   giving to light.

I was my mother's gift to the sun of her life.

She revolved around my father,
the classic distant satellite
that came close enough to eclipse her once a year.

But that year, the one I was born, he was busy
in New York City. Wired us money & a name in his stead.
Told Mamá to call me Camino.

Sixteen years ago, the day I was born, was light-filled.
Tía has told me so. It is the only birthday Papi ever missed.
A bright July day. But it seems this year he'll miss it too.

Because the people at the airport are wailing, crying,
hands cast up: it fell, they say. It fell.
They say   the plane fell right out the sky.

———————

It's always been safer to listen to Papi's affection
than it is to bear his excuses. Easier to shine
in his being here than bring up the shadow of his absence.

Every year for my birthday he asks me what I want.
Since the year my mother died, I've always answered:
"To live with you. In the States."

I've heard him tell of New York so often you'd think
I was born to that skyline. Sometimes it feels like I have
memories of his billiards, Tío's colmado, Yankee Stadium,

as if they are places I grew up at,
& not just the tall tales he's been sharing
since I was a chamaquita on his knee.

In the fall, I start senior year at the International School.
My plan has always been to apply to
& attend Columbia University.

I told Papi last year this dream of premed,
at that prestigious university, in the heart of the city
that he calls home. & he laughed.

He said I could be a doctor here. He said
it'd be better for me to visit Colombia the country
than for him to spend money at another fancy school.

I did not laugh with him. He must have realized
his laugh was like one of those paper shredders
making a sad confetti of my hopes.

He did not apologize.

———

It is a mistake, I know.
A plane did not crash.
My father's plane did not fall.

& if, *if*, a plane did fall
of course my father
could not have been on it.

He would have known
that metal husk was ill-fated.
Tía's Saints would have warned him.

It would be like in the movies,
where the taxi makes a wrong turn,
or mysteriously the alarm does not go off

& Papi would be scrambling
to get to the airport only to learn
he had been saved. Saved.

This is what I think the whole long walk home.
For four miles I scan the road & ignore
catcalls. I know Don Mateo would come back to get me

if I called, but I feel frozen from
the inside out. The only things working
are my feet moving forward & my mind

outracing my feet.

I create scenario after scenario;
I damn everyone else on that flight
but save my father in my imagination.

I ignore the news alerts
coming through on my phone.
I do not check social media.

Once I get to my callejón,
I smile at the neighbors
& blow kisses at Vira Lata.

It isn't true, you see?
My father was *not* on that plane.
I refuse.

———

Papi boards the same flight every year.

Tía & I are like the hands of a clock:
we circle our purpose around his arrival.
We prepare for his exaggerated stories

of businesspeople who harrumph over tomato juice
& flight attendants who sneak winks at him.
He never sleeps on flights, instead plays chess on his tablet.

He got me one for my birthday last year,
& before he boarded his flight this morning
we video-chatted.

They're saying it's too early to know about survivors.

I am so accustomed to his absence
that this feels more like delay than death.
By the time I get home, Tía has heard the news.

She holds me tight & rocks me back & forth,
I do not join her in moaning *ay ay ay*.
I am stiff as a soiled rag that's been left in the sun.

Tía says I'm in shock. & I think she is right.
I feel just like I've been struck by lightning.
When a neighbor arrives, Tía lets me go.

I sit on el balcón & rock myself in Papi's favorite chair.

When Tía goes to bed, I go stand in front of the altar
she's dedicated to our ancestors. It's an old chest, covered
in white cloth that sits behind our dining room table.

It's one of the places where we pray & put our offerings.
I sneak one of the cigars Tía has left there. I carefully cut
the tip, strike a match, & for a moment consider kissing

that small blue flame. I lift my mouth to the cigar. Inhale.
Hold the smoke hard in my lungs
until the pain squeezes sharp in my chest

& I cough & cough & cough,
gasping for breath,
tears springing to my eyes.

I rock rock rock until the sun creaks over the tree line.
I listen for the whine of a taxi motor,
for Papi's loud bark of a laugh, his air-disrupting voice

saying how damn happy
he is to finally be home—
Knowing I'll never hear any of his sounds again.

———

CAMINO ✈ YAHAIRA

When you learn life-altering news
you're often in the most basic of places.

I am at lunch, sitting in the corner with Andrea—
or Dre, although I'm the only person who calls her that.

She is telling me about the climate-change protest
while I flip through a magazine.

Dre is outlining where she'll be meeting the organizers
& the demands they'll be making at city hall

when Ms. Santos's crackling voice
pushes through the loudspeaker:

Yahaira Rios. Yahaira Rios.
Please report to the main office.

I feel every eye in the cafeteria turn to me.
I hand the magazine to Dre, reminding her

not to dog-ear any of the pages
since it belongs to the library.

I grab a pass from the teacher on lunch duty,
but Mr. Henry, the security guard,

smiles when I flash it his way,

"I heard them call you, girl.
Not like you would be cutting nohow."

I hold back a sigh. On the chessboard
I used to be known for my risk taking.

But in real life? I'm predictable:

I follow directions when they are given
& rarely break the rules.

I hang out every Saturday with Dre,
watching Netflix or reading fashion blogs

or if she's in charge of our entertainment,
watching gardening tutorials on YouTube

(which I pretend to understand
simply because anything she loves

I love to watch her watch).

Teachers' progress reports
always have the same comments:

Quiet in class, shows potential,
needs to apply more effort.

I am a rule follower. A person whose
report card always says *Meets Expectations*.

I do not exceed them. I do not do poorly.
I arrive & mind my business.

So I have no idea what anyone in the main office
could possibly want with me.

How could I have guessed the truth of it?
Even as teachers in the halls gasped as the news spread,

even as the main office was surrounded by parents
& guidance counselors. How could I have known then

there are no rules, no expectations, no rising to the occasion.
When you learn news like this, there is only

falling.

———

I replay that moment again & again,
circle it like a plane in a holding pattern.

How that morning, on the fifth day of June,
the worst thing I could imagine

was being lectured for my progress report
or getting another nudge to return to the chess club.

I didn't know then that three hours before,
as I'd arrived at school,

before lunch or Dre or the long walk down the school hallway,
the door to my old life slammed shut.

———

When I walk into the office, Mami is here.
Wearing chancletas, her hair in rollers.

& that's the move that telegraphs the play:

Mami manages a nice spa uptown
& says her polished appearance is advertisement.

She never leaves the house anything less
than Ms. Universe–perfect.

The principal's assistant, Ms. Santos,
comes from around her desk,

puts an arm around my shoulders.
She looks like she's been weeping.

I want to shake her arm off.
Want to shove her back to her desk.

That arm is trying to tell me
something I don't have the stomach to hear.

I don't want her comfort. Don't want
Mami here, or anything about what's to come.

I take a breath, the way I used to
before I walked into a room

where every single person
wanted to see me lose. "Ma?"

When she looks at me, I notice her eyes
are red & puffy, her bottom lip quivers,

& she presses the tips of her fingers there
as if to create a wall against the sob that threatens.

She answers, "Tu papi."

———

The flight

Papi was on departs
without incident on most days, I'm told.

Leaves from JFK International Airport & lands
in Puerto Plata in exactly three hours & thirty-six minutes.

Routine, I'm told, a routine flight, with the same kind of plane that flies in
daily & gets a mechanical check & had a veteran pilot & should have

                                                    landed fine.

Mami says the panic hit most of the waiting families at the same time.
Here, in New York, with the Atlantic refereeing between us,

we knew much earlier. Thirty minutes after the plane
departed, it was reported that the tail had snapped,

that like some fishing, hunting creature
the jet plunged into the water

completely vertical, hungry
for only God knows

what—prey.

Sank.

———

I sign myself out of school.
Ignore Ms. Santos's condolences.

Mami is still crying.
We walk to my locker.

I leave my books in the cafeteria.
Mami is still crying.

I leave school without saying goodbye to Dre.
Mami can't stop crying.

Mr. Henry waves. I wave back.
Outside the day is beautiful.

Mami cries.
The sun is shining.

The breeze a soft touch along my face.
Mami is still crying.

It's almost as if the day has forgotten
it's stolen my father   or maybe it's rejoicing at its gain.

Mami is still crying,
but my eyes? They remain dry.

———

I learn via text I am one of four students at school
who had been called to the office because of the flight.

In the neighborhood, las vecinas are on their stoops
in their batas & chancletas,

everyone trying to learn
what the TV may not know:

Who was on the flight? Is it true everyone is dead?
Was it terrorists? A conspiracy de por allá? The government?

When the women call out to Mami
she does not turn her head their way.

We walk from the school to our apartment
as if we are the ones who have been made ghosts.

The bodegueros & Danilo the tailor
& the other store owners

stand outside their shops
making phone calls as viejitos

wring their hands in front of their bellies
& shake their heads.

Here in Morningside Heights,
we are a mix of people: Dominicans

& Puerto Ricans & Haitians,
Black Americans & Riverside Drive white folk,

& of course, the Columbia students
who disrupt everything: clueless to our joys & pains.

But those of us from the island
will all know someone who died on that flight.

When we get to our building,
Doña Gonzalez from the fifth floor

calls out from her window,
pero Mami does not look up,

does not look sideways, does not stop
until we walk through our apartment door,

& then, as if pierced, she deflates,
slides down to the floor

with her head in her hands, & I watch
as the rollers slip free one by one, as her body shakes

& she unravels. I do not slide down to join her.

Instead, I put my arms underneath hers,
help her up to her feet & into her bedroom.

When the phone begins ringing
I answer & murmur to family.

I take charge where no one else can.

———

Last summer, when I learned my father's secret,
it was like bank-style gates descended on my tongue:

no words could escape. Those words I learned
must be protected at all cost. Even from my family.

Papi thought my silence was because of chess.
Because I was angry at his disapproval.

He never once imagined that my silence
was my disappointment in him. At what I'd found.

But although I felt he'd become a stranger,
I never stopped being my parents' steady daughter.

Who did her chores & bothered no one.
Even now, that is not a habit I know how to break.

I take down the trash. I microwave the leftovers.
I wrap myself tight around the feelings I cannot share,

an unopened present, a gift no one wants.

———

CAMINO ✈ YAHAIRA

One Day After

The day after the crash,

but with still no deaths confirmed,
my friend Carline comes by before work,
hugs me tightly, her swollen belly between us,

but I quickly pull away.
I am afraid that I would break her.
Am afraid that I would break.

She is quiet. Holds my hand in hers. Says God
will see me through. Carline has lost aunts & uncles
& cousins & knows about mourning,

but she still has both parents at home. & so,
I take her comfort without yelling
that she Does. Not. Understand.

When her phone buzzes, she quickly releases
my hand on a curse. I know without her telling me
it's her manager at the resort, wondering where she is.

When she leaves, Tía sits in front of the TV
& Don Mateo comes over, hat in his hands, & the phone rings, &
even Vira Lata, usually mellow, howls at our gate.

Everyone in these streets knew Papi:
The hustlers he gave money to keep an eye on me,
the colmado owners & fruit-cart guys who held our tab,

the folks Tía has been a curandera to, healing their babies.
The neighbor women send pastelones & papayas,
& men stop by to offer care in the form of labor & prayer.

Papi was gone three-fourths of each year but kept his ear
pressed to the ground all three hundred sixty-five days.
& so, like grains of rice in boiling water,

the crowd outside our little teal house expands.
People stand there in shorts & caps,
in thong sandals, the viejos held up by their bastones,

they shuffle onto the balcón,
they wrap their fingers around the barred fence,
they watch & wait & watch & wait   an unrehearsed vigil.

& they pray   & I try not to suffocate
under all the eyes that seem to be expecting
me to tear myself out of my skin.

———

We have the nicest house in the barrio
because Papi spent money to make it so.
He wanted to move us, but Tía refused

to leave the neighborhood she knows & serves.
So instead, Papi got us fat iron locks,
running water, & a working bathroom we don't have to share.

We have humming air conditioners,
a large refrigerator, & a small microwave.
A generator para cuando se va la luz,

the latter setting us apart;
when the daily power outages happen
& the whole hood goes dark,

we are one of the few homes with our lights still on.
But it feels like for the first time,
our house is the one that's gone dim.

————

Our house is squat, with two bedrooms,
a kitchen & comedor.
A small patio in the backyard where we hold

prayer circles & parties.
Our floors are not dirt. But tiled recently,
& always mopped clean.

We have a TV in the living room,
& Wi-Fi, & so many small luxuries
Papi's US sweat provided.

But the best thing about our house
is that it's a three-minute walk from the beach.
Which isn't always lucky when the water rises,

but it has saved my life on the many days
when I need a reminder the world is bigger
than the one I know, & its currents are always moving;

when I need a reminder
there is a life for me beyond the water
& that one day I will not be left behind.

———◆———

My bathing suit is a red-hot color,
like the one from that old North American show *Baywatch*?
Not as low cut. Unfortunately.

I sneak out of the house through the back
& avoid the well-meaning people out front,
whose questions & condolences I want to swat.

From the back road, it's a straight shot to the water's edge.
Even though I snuck out from the back, Vira Lata is soon
dogging my feet.

I pass a couple of houses & two bar fronts
where men play dominoes & sip lukewarm beer.
This is the edge of our neighborhood.

El Cero sits outside one bar in his blue shorts,
his eyes following me as I approach. He is a man
somewhere older than me but younger than Papi,

& I've known that from the moment I turned thirteen
Papi paid El Cero a yearly fee to leave me alone.
But the last few months, I've felt his eyes on my back.

Little things, like him now hanging outside my bus stop.
Or strolling more often on the beach. Carline even told me
she saw him at the resort once & he asked about me.

I keep *my* eyes on the road as I walk past.
I hunch myself invisible. & then my favorite sight:
the thicket of trees, & small path through them,

then the embankment of well-worn dirt
that gives way to sun-bleached sand.
This nook is bookended by jagged cliffs on one side—

that's where the chamaquitos dive—& on the other is the
stone wall that separates the neighborhood from the resort
where Carline works.

I avoid the cliff; I am not here to leap & flip.
I am here because I need the current, moving & steady
& never the same twice. Rolling clear & blue right where I left it.

My small oasis. Papi used to call it Camino's Playa.
The water-babble rushes my worst thoughts quiet.
& I peel my denim shorts off, wade in, slicing through

as if by doing this I could cut to strips my breaking heart.

———◆———

Swimming might be the closest to flying
a human being can get. There is something
about your body displacing water

in order to propel through space that makes you feel
Godtouched. That makes me understand evolution,
that we really must have crawled up from the sea.

My life's passions
are all about water breaking, new life making,
taking breath in wrinkled flesh.

Tía tells me I am probably the daughter
of a water saint. All I know is I am most sure
of my place in the world

with the water combing my kinks,
the cold biting into my skin, & my arms
creating an arc over my head as I barrel through,

& battle too   these elements.

———◆———

Papi learned to swim in this cut of the Caribbean Sea.
Used to jump off the cliffs into the waiting blue.
When I was younger, he gave me lessons,

scoffing at the placidness of the nearby resort pool.
"Buenooo, the best way to learn to swim,
is to jump into a body of water that wants to kill you."

It used to be funny when he said that.
Most days, he would watch from the sand
as I tried to become a thing with fins.

Some days, he'd strip off his shirt,
show off his hairy chest & jiggly belly,
& make me want to disown him on the spot.

The other barrio kids watched as "el Papi de Camino,"
the one who brought her cool shirts from the States,
would slide off his old-man sandals & hat, walk to a little peak,

& execute a dive, entering the water so smoothly
it would make el Michael Phelps jealous.
In those moments, Papi became a lago creature,

a human knife, a merman
from some ocean mythology—
so smooth I would search his neck for gills.

There was no current strong enough
that could pull against his push.
I am convinced Papi was made up of more water than most.

The little kids would cheer & try to climb his back,
so he would become a human surfboard too, & I would
say, "Ese es mi papi; he is mine all mine."

Papi learned to swim in water that wanted to kill him.
That ocean can't be so different; shouldn't be any different.
If any man could take a hard dive & come up breathing,

it should be one who had practiced for just that his entire life.

———

My arms are tired, my joints screaming. I want to swim
until I become this water. The world fades when you are
under, & the ocean murmurs *stay stay stay*.

I swim out & come back, out & come back.
My lungs on fire. My arms shaking from the strain.
I could stop moving. I could just   go.

I turn my head to breathe; a sharp whistle cuts me off midstroke.
Floating on my back, eyes opening to the darkening sky,
I do not have to look to know the figure at the shore.

"It's getting late, Camino. The beach is dangerous at night."
El Cero. In some ways it seems like I always knew
that Papi's absence would bring baggage.

I tread upright in the water, trying to map out
the fastest escape route to get by El Cero
without having to go near him. Vira Lata wags his tail at me.

I wish he was more inclined to bare his teeth.

Even from a distance, I see El Cero's eyes dip down
to where my nipples are cold as I tread.
& I know, the most dangerous thing on this beach

has nothing to do with the dark.
The most dangerous thing
is standing right in front of me.

———

El Cero is not a man to be trusted. Or a man to show fear.
Without lowering my head, I calmly walk past him,
snatch my shorts up, & suck my teeth in his direction.

Vira Lata must read my mood.
He comes over to rub against my leg,
& I pat him once to let him know I'm all right.

I want nothing to do with the crowing roosters,
or the viejos lighting candles, & Tía watching the news,
& people crowding the patio,

& the prayer circles, & the watchful eyes, &
the whispers about Papi being dead.
But whatever it is El Cero wants from me

I know it will be worse
than the momentary discomfort at Tía's house.
Because El Cero will attach conditions to his condolences.

———————

Papi didn't like that I've had boys
flirting with me since I was twelve,
but he would have had to be around

to stop them, or to keep me
from flirting back. Plus he was never
as strict as he pretended.

I don't mess with dudes from the barrio
who love gossiping at the domino bars
about the girls that they've slept with.

I usually only flirt
with the international boys from school.
The ones with American accents,

their blue passports & blue blood
both stamped with prestige & money;
those are the boys I switch my hips at.

Not because they're cute or interesting—
they're often obnoxious & only want a taste
of my gutter-slick tongue & brownness;

they act as if they could elevate my life with a
taste of their powder-milk-tinged pomp.
No, I date those boys because they are safe.

They can't dance bachata or sing Juan Luis Guerra,
can't recite Salomé Ureña or even name the forefathers;
they wrap their flag around their shoulders like a safety blanket,

& if a heart has topography,
I know none of these boys know the coordinates
to navigate & survive mine's rough terrain.

In other words, these boys would be no distraction.

———

Papi was a tiguerazo.
A hustler. A no-nonsense street-smart guy.
He could sell water to a fire hydrant,

sell a lit match to a burning gas station.
Papi comes from here: Sosúa, Puerto Plata,
República Dominicana. & he's always said

he never wanted me or my tía
to polish boots or sell lottery tickets, to know
hunger or the anger of going without.

& so our poor isn't as poor as our neighbors'.
But it definitely isn't as rich as my classmates'.
It's the poor of an American sponsorship.

The poor of relying on Western Union
& a busy father & money that mostly goes to tuition;
the poor of secondhand Nikes, leather repainted to look new.

Papi was a hustler: a first cousin to sweat,
a criado of hard work. A king who built an empire
so I'd have a throne to inherit.

———

El Cero is not the kind of hustler Papi was.
El Cero hustles bodies;   eagle-eyes young girls
from the time they are ten   & gets them

in his pocket with groceries & a kind word.
When those girls develop & show the
bud of a blossom, he plucks them for his team.

& although most people here won't admit they think like me,
a woman should be able to sell whatever she wants to sell.
But *not* if it's at the insistence of a man. This man.

Word on the street is El Cero always gets a first taste
of the girls who work for him. Before he gussies them up
& takes them by the resort beach in cut-off tanks & short shorts

so the men from all over the world who come here for sun
& sex can give thumbs-up or -down to his wares. His women.
Not women, yet. Girls.

So, no. El Cero is not the kind of hustler Papi was.

He has no code.
The sweat that makes his money is not his own.
Even now, as I stare at the setting sun & walk away,

he calls out, "Camino, you know, I'm here for you.
Whatever you need. Some extra money, or a shoulder
to cry on. Just let me know. Your father's life, it's such a loss."

It is a warm evening. But my skin feels kissed by cold.

Whatever Papi was paying him each year I think El Cero
is still expecting. Even though I don't have a dime
to my name. I know there are other ways he'd accept payment.

I know he would love nothing more
than to have me further
in his debt.

———

I know what El Cero sees when he looks at me:
This hair, the curls down my back,
lightened by sun & always tangled.

This thin body, better fed than most, curved softly
in the places that elicit dog whistles & piropos; swimming
has kept this body honed like Tía's oft-sharpened machete.

I am pointy angles: knees & elbows,
sharp cheekbones & jaw, jagged tongue—
although the last is not the water's fault.

My skin is the same color as Tía's, as Mamá's.
If Papi's photo was shot in black & white,
I would be cast in soft sepia: shades of golden brown.

I am a girl who does not look like a woman.
I am a girl who looks like a girl.
I am a girl who is not full-fledged   yet.

& that's exactly what El Cero counts on.
A girl, easy to convince into a trade she doesn't want,
easy to sell to the men who do.

———

I used to go to school with El Cero's little sister.
Back then he wasn't El Cero yet. He was just
skinny Alejandro, Emily's older brother.

Back before the fever that swept in with a hurricane.
Back before the deaths, the illness.
Back before Papi put me in private school. Back before it all.

Cero's little sister had a big gap-toothed smile,
a gap that wasn't just because we were both seven
& missing teeth.

              Cero's little sister was my friend.
The first to raise her hand in class, to volunteer
to read out loud. She waved at everyone & everything:

the pregnant gutter cats, the women
who sold ointments & socks, the drunkards on the
corner singing off-key.

The dengue fever came with the rain.
Tía didn't have enough hands to try to heal them all.
Not even her own stubborn sister who said she was fine.

Not the little girl who was her niece's
good friend. There were lots of funerals
that October. Rumor is, after Cero's sister died

he was never the same. Before I learned to fear him,
there was one memory that kept coming back,
the one I cannot shake even as I shake when he approaches:

Cero has never appeared young to me. Always this same
age, this same face. But he would come to school
to pick Emily up. & she would stop

everything she was doing & run to him, arms spread wide.
He would catch her, swinging her in circles. & I was jealous.
Jealous I didn't have a consistent male figure like Cero in my
    life.

———

Tía has kept the TV on since the accident.
She hasn't blown out the three big candles
under a picture of my father

on the ancestral altar.
This morning, divers began
pulling up pieces of the plane.

Papi loved the water, could hold his breath
longer than anyone. The news coverage has died down;
they say any chance of survivors has too.

It's been seventy-two hours, & I go to school on Monday
even though Tía tells me I should stay home. I want normal.
But my teachers do not ask me for homework, do not ask me
        questions.

In the afternoon, El Cero sits on a crate
near where my bus drops me off. Later he is outside the
bar I have to walk past to get to the beach.

I try not to dread that he seems to appear on every corner.
But it feels like El Cero has sullied any sense of safety.
& since most of his dealings happen at the resort next door,

I know that he won't be leaving me or this sand alone;
like a too-skinny cat who knows you hold scraps
in one hand & a smack in the other, I give him a wide berth.

For dinner, I warm the days-old stew that I still can't stomach.
At this point, we have no reason to hope but I can't say the
    words
because then it will become   real.

———————

Tía & I both act
like not talking about it
will make it not true.

I help her grind & dry
herbs. We mend towels
& watch TV quietly.

Once or twice when I walk
into the living room, I hear her
murmuring on the phone;

she's always quick to hang up;
I think she's been making
funeral arrangements

but knows she can't tell me. Knows
my shoulders are too narrow
to bear that news just yet.

———

CAMINO ✈ YAHAIRA

Some people play chess, but I *played* chess.
Not like your abuelito at the park plays chess.

No offense to anybody's grandfather. It's just,
my ranking's more official than your abuelito's.

Last year my FIDE ranking was higher
than the year I was born, well over the 2000s.

I scrubbed kids weekly at citywide competitions
& was on a travel team for national tournaments.

Until last year.

I'm not the best student at A. C. Portalatín High School,
but I was one of the best chess players in the entire city.

& I ensured our team won titles,
& the school loved me for it; so did the neighborhood.

I got us into the newspapers & on late-night TV
for something other than drugs or poor test scores or
        gentrification.

But last year, things changed. & so did I.
So did chess. & if the game taught me one thing,

it's once you lift a pawn off the board,
you have to move it forward. It cannot return where it was.

———

Papi was a good chess teacher.
He was not a good chess player.

Evidenced by how terribly he hid things.
You could always tell his next play.

At least, that's what I used to think.

When Papi is in DR we do not speak often,
but I never had to reach him

the way I did one day last summer.
It felt like he might be

the only person to help me make sense
of The Thing That Happened.

The thing I still find hard to talk about.
I called his cell. He didn't answer.

I sent him a text, & no response.
I tried his email, but one day later

my inbox was still empty.

I realized Papi always travels for negocios,
but I didn't have a single work number.

I called Tío Jorge to ask, but he
said he didn't have a phone to call.

Mami rubbed my back but said
Papi would get to me when he could.

On a day Mami wasn't home, I went through
a folder of Papi's papers. I thought one of his

business forms might have a company number.
My fingers, drawn like magnets, landed on a closed envelope.

I know Mami had never
looked at it herself.

I know this for a fact because if she had
she would know what I now know,

what she cannot know
or nothing would have been like it was.

———

It depends on whether Mami or Papi
is telling it, their story.

According to Papi, he saw Mami
at El Malecón in Puerto Plata.

Sitting near the water's edge,
rocking high-waist jeans,

"Guapa y alta como un modelo.
Straight hair & the nose of a Roman empress."

According to Mami,
she saw Papi creeping closer.

Dark like the skin of a vanilla bean,
a barrel chest & the hands of a mechanic.

"Fuerte como un luchador.
Pelo afro y esos dientes derechitos."

According to Papi, Mami looked fina,
like a porcelain chess piece to be captured.

According to Mami,
something about him called to her.

Maybe his laugh, scattering birds as it rang out.
The way the crowd parted as he walked toward her,

the way she stood & watched, unfazed & half smiling,
forcing him to puff up his chest,

to smooth his hair, to introduce himself to the woman
he said he'd one day wife.

———

You would think
coffee & condensed milk

would give you some kind
of light brown.

But I came out Papi's mirror,
his bella negra.

Thick hair like his,
thick lips like his,

thick skin like his.
When some of my cousins

from Mami's side
dissed me la prieta fea,

I never listened. Papi's
reminder in my ear:

you are dark
& always been beautiful:

like the night, like a star after it bursts,
like obsidian & onyx & jet   precious.

But I know I am beautiful
like all & none of those things:

far in the sky & deep in the earth
I am beautiful like a dark-skinned girl that is right here.

I've always preferred playing black
on the chessboard.

Always advancing,
conquering my offending

other side.

———

But although I got Papi's skin color
& his facial features, my body

is all Mami's. Her curves are a road map
for my own dips.

You cannot say I am not both their child.
The first time Dre touched me

without our clothes on, she kept running her hand
from waist to hip. & I wanted to write Mami

a thank-you text, for giving my body a spot
that was made to nest Dre's hand.

Sometimes I look down at my fingers,
& they are long & thin;

it's Mami's imprint
covered in my father's dark.

But my laugh is an interrupter,
all Papi. The cock of my head: all him.

When it comes to personality,
I am neither one of them.

When they hold boisterous family parties,
I'd rather be reading in my room.

Where Papi is always thinking
of how to save another dollar,

I'm dreaming up a Sephora wish list
to request for my next birthday.

Mami stands in front of a stove for hours,
& I would burn an untoasted sandwich.

I am theirs. You can see them on me.
But I am also all mine,   mostly.

———

Three Days After

Because I don't know
if Papi is an anchor

at the bottom of the ocean,
I ignore everyone's calls.

I press Decline on my phone
as classmates hit me up.

I want to fold my ears
like empty candy wrappers,

small & small & smaller
until no words fit inside.

I'm afraid if I close my eyes
I will have accepted

his will never open again.
It is a losing battle;

I fall asleep on the couch
with the remote in my hand.

I am awakened by a moan
that sounds like something monstrous

has clawed its way into my mother's body.

Her ear cradles the house phone
but my eyes follow hers to the TV:

There have been no survivors found from flight 1112.

———————

Dre has been my best friend
since her family rented the apartment next door.

She's been my girlfriend
since some time during seventh grade.

We share a fire escape,
& the summer we turned twelve

we found ourselves out there
at the same hours of the day.

Dre would be reading a fantasy novel
or pruning a half-dead tomato plant,

& I'd be playing chess on my phone,
or looking at nail tutorials.

She & I became tight
as freshly laundered jeans.

Both of us absorbed in our own worlds
but comfortable sharing space.

Dre comes from a Southern military family.
She wasn't meant to be a hippie child,

but she's granola to the core. A tree-hugging,
squirrel-feeding, astrology-following vegan.

Me? I was a fashion-loving, chess-playing negrita
who quit at the top of my game.

We both know what it's like to have our parents look at us
like we are dressed in neon question marks.

We also know exactly what it's like to look at the other
& see all the answers of ourselves there.

———

I am a girl who will notice
if your nostril hair grows long

or if your nails are cut too close to the quick.
I'd as soon compliment you

on how well you groom your edges
as I would on how smoothly you steer a debate.

Dre will turn any conversation
into one about gardening.

If you tell a dirty joke,
Dre will talk about plants that pollinate themselves.

If you talk about hoing around,
you'd see Dre blink as her mind goes down a

long winding path of tilling dirt & sowing seeds.
Here we are, with our interests in chess

& astrology & dirt & each other.

———◆———

Dre has been texting me
since this morning.

She must have seen the news.
She didn't hear it from me

because I turned off my phone.
The thought of speaking

makes me want to
uncarve myself from this skin.

But you can only ignore
your girlfriend for so long

before she knocks on the window

& sticks her head in.
"Is it true, Yaya?"

& I hear the tremble
in her voice

that threatens the wobble
in my own.

Dre loved Papi
as if he were her own family.

Would make Papi laugh
with her precise school Spanish

& North Carolina manners.
"I don't know, Dre.

Anything is possi—"
I stop myself midway.

It feels like such a lie.
Nothing & no one feels possible anymore.

I cannot see her nodding.
But I know that she is.

I know that tears are streaming
down her clay-brown cheeks.

She tucks her long legs through
the window & folds herself onto the floor,

rests her head against my knee
& hugs my legs.

"I'm here, Yaya. I'm here."
For hours we sit. Just like that.

———

Dre is originally from Raleigh.
& although she's lived in New York

for a long time, every now & then
her accent will switch up.

Especially when she's upset
or hurting or trying to be strong.

When New Yorkers are mad?
Our words take on an edge,

we speed talk like relay racers
struggling to pass the baton to the next snide phrase.

But Dre, when she's upset, her words slow down,
& she becomes even more polite, & I know then

she is Dr. Johnson's child through & through.
Dr. Johnson takes on that same precise & calm manner,

her words an unrolling ribbon that you aren't sure
you'll see the end of.

When Dr. Johnson is upset, her hands fold
in front of her stomach, & her head cocks to the side

as she lectures us on why we should have finished
our homework sooner, or why a certain movie or social-media
    clip

wasn't actually as funny as we thought
if we put it in a larger context.

Mr. Johnson, or should I say, Senior Master Sergeant Johnson,
is in the Air Force. I've only met him a handful of times,

& he didn't talk enough for me to evaluate how quick or slow,
how calm or angry the pacing of his speech was.

But Dre speaks to me slowly. Like I've seen her
whisper to a drooping plant. Believing that her own breath

can unfurl a dying leaf. Can sing it back to health.
Can unwilt the stalk.

———————

The summer before seventh grade,
Dre grew tall. When extended completely,

her legs stretched beyond the bars
of the fire escape & hung over the edge

like Jordan-clad pigeon perches.
Dre wants to study speech therapy in college,

but I've always thought she should do agriculture.
I've never seen anyone make as much grow

in a small pot on a fire escape as I've seen
Dre coax small seeds to bud & flower here.

She has a railing planter where she grows okra;
on our side of the fire escape, which gets better light,

she's planted tomatoes. One time she planted
these little peppers that came out green & spicy.

Although the landlord has sent notices
that her fire-escape nursery is a fire hazard,

Dre just figures out another way to stack her plants,
or hang them on the railing, or hide them in plain sight,

so she can blossom. Even when the pigeons pick at her
seedlings, or squirrels munch on fresh shoots,

Dre just laughs & puts her black hands back in the soil:
decides to grow us   something   good.

———

Papi never saw what Dre
& I were to each other. At least,

he never mentioned it.
Ma is more watchful.

& it's not that Ma did not like
that I liked Dre. It's that she understood

I wanted no big deal to be made.

There is an artist my mother loved,
Juan Gabriel, who was once asked

in an interview if he was gay.
His reply: What's understood need not be said.

I remember how Mami's eyes
fluttered to me

like a bee on a flower
acknowledging the pollen is sweet.

I have never had to tell
Mami I like girls.

She knew. & she knew that Dre was special.
Last year, for Valentine's Day, before I left for school,

Mami handed me an envelope
with a twenty-dollar bill inside,

stirring a pot of something fragrant
while she said, "Pa que le compre algo nice a Andreita."

With her, I did not have to pretend
my best friend was just a friend.

———————

The girl next door being the girl for you
is the kind of trope my English teacher

would have us write essays about in class.
But that's how it happened for Dre & me.

One day we were best friends,
& the next day we were best friends

who stared at each other's mouths
when we shared lip gloss.

I don't think I understood the word
W   O   N   D   E   R

until the day our tongues touched
& we both wanted

to have them touch again. This girl
felt about me   how I felt about her.

The day we first kissed,
I walked into my parents' bedroom

& offered thanks to the little porcelain saint
Papi kept on his armoire:

                    thank you, thank you.
I whispered to everything that listened.

The only thing about Dre
that gets on my nerves

is that Dre is sometimes
too good. She has a scale

for doing what's right
that always balances out

nice & evenly for her.
Which is why she was

so disappointed that I
didn't "come out" in

the way she wanted me to.
She said we shouldn't hide

what we are to each other.
& I told her I wasn't hiding,

I just wasn't making
a loudspeaker announcement

to my parents or anyone.
People who know me, know.

Dre's quirks come out
in other ways too.

Sometimes Dre wants me
to have a clear opinion

on plastic straws, or
water rights, or my feelings

about Papi, & she doesn't
always see I need time

to watch the board,
to come to terms with

the possibilities.

———

I'm telling you about my skin,
& my home, & mostly about Dre,

because it's easier than telling you
Papi   is   dead.

If I say those words,
if I snap apart the air with them,

whatever is binding me together
will split too.

———➤———

The house phone has been ringing
off the hook all day.

Reporters from American
& Latin American channels

& newspapers & magazines
& podcasts & websites.

Family members
from the Bronx & DR.

The neighborhood association,
which invites us to grief counseling,

special sessions that will be
held at the church.

The phone rings & rings,
& Mami's voice,

raw as unprocessed sugar,
responds & responds

but does not answer
where we'll go from here.

———

Here is a thing that no one knows,
& probably wouldn't believe if I told them.

The night before Papi got on the plane,
I almost asked him not to go.

It would have been the first full sentence
I'd spoken to him in almost a year.

We haven't been close, not like we were,
since I stopped playing chess,

since he tried to force me to go back,
since I saw the certificate in the sealed envelope.

When I quit playing chess,
he told me I broke his heart.

I never told him he'd broken mine.
In the Dominican Republic,

before he met Mami & came here
& started this life for us

Papi was an accountant,
a man of numbers & money,

but here he hustled his way into
owning a billiards on Dyckman Street.

I don't believe in magic
or premonitions. Not like Papi,

who crossed himself every time he left the house.
Not like Mami, who tries to interpret dreams.

But on the night before Papi left for DR,
something yanked on my heart,

& I wanted to ask him to stay.
But I never said the words.

& Papi did something
he hadn't done in over a year:

came to my room to say good night

& tangled his hand in my hair
while I was two-strand twisting my curls.

I *hate* when he messes up my fresh wash,
but I also missed him. My fingers caught in his. Held.

Before I moved away. Removed myself from his reach.
"Me tengo que ir, los negocios. Ya tú sabes."

He's always back right before my birthday in September,
but every year around this time,

Mami's spine becomes rigid, her lips pulled tight
as sneaker laces biting into the tongue.

As his departure nears it seems like I can see
the space between my parents stretch & grow.

& she refuses to drive him to the airport
despite how much I beg her so that I can be there when he leaves.

Papi stopped trying to joke her out of her ill humor years ago,
& I wonder if she now regrets that his last few days

here, at home, alive,
were spent in bed with her anger.

I did not reply to him. Whenever he left,
he said it was for business. I now knew he was lying.

He fiddled with the light switch in my room.

"Negra bella, te quiero. I know things haven't been normal
between us, but I hope when I come back, we can talk about it."

I peeked at him from the mirror
while my fingers twirled & twirled my hair.

I remember how I started to say something,
then yanked the words before they could get loose.

He shook his head as if changing his mind.
"While I'm gone, cúidate, negra."

& I never said a word.

———

Once, when I was still young to chess competitions,
I was in a tournament with all older kids.

I'd made it to one of the last rounds
& had been playing well the whole time.

I was convinced I was going to win the whole thing.
But I missed an opponent's trap & was put in check.

My hands shook, tears welled up in my eyes,
the clock kept ticking, but I wouldn't move.

When I finally looked up, I could see Papi watching
through the glass of the double doors.

He didn't blink, he didn't shake his head,
he didn't do anything, but somehow I knew.

I straightened my back; I wiped my eyes.
I knocked down my king.

The train ride home was silent.
But before we got off at our stop,

Papi turned to my nine-year-old self & said:
"Never, ever, let them see you sweat, negra.

Fight until you can't breathe, & if you have to forfeit,
you forfeit smiling, make them think you let them win."

Four Days After

on the news

blunt force

trauma on impact

medical examiner

unidentifiable

extreme forces

not intact

unconfirmed

dental records

anthropological forensics

tattoos   fingerprints

teeth   personal items

———◆———

I watch video footage
of the plane spearing into the ocean.

The waves rising   open arms   welcome.
I wait for news that the passengers

got their life jackets on.
That there were previously unreported life rafts.

That their initial assessment was wrong
That the Coast Guard found someone breathing.

The news only repeats the same words:
No survivors found. The number of dead: unconfirmed.

Where the plane went down is 120 feet deep.
Divers have been jumping into the water,

fifteen-minute intervals at a time,
trying to pull up what might be left.

I tell Mami we need to go to Queens,
the closest shore to where the plane fell.

Dozens of people have been lighting candles
by the water. The small hope inside me is illogical.

I know this. But it urges me to go. If I
can just be as close as possible to the crash site,

my presence might change the outcome.
All Mami does is drag herself to her room

where she denies   my request
with a sharp but quiet *click*.

———

Papi sat me in front of a chessboard
when I was three years old.

He patiently explained all the pieces,
but I still treated each one like a pawn.

He loved . . . *loves* to tell the story
of how I would give up my king

all willy-nilly but would protect my knight
because "Me gustan los caballitos!"

(In my defense, why would a three-year-old
pick a dry-ass-looking king over a pony?)

But even when I was bored, I was also good
at memorizing the patterns for openings

& closings, for when to castle & when to capture.
I was fascinated by the rhythm of the game;

it came as naturally to my body as when Papi
taught me how to dance. It's all just steps & patterns.

By the time I was four,
I could beat Papi if he wasn't paying attention.

On my fifth birthday, I defeated him
in just six moves.

After that, he would take me downtown on the C train
to compete against the Washington Square Park hustlers

who played for money. They were straight sharks
& thought the little girl too cute to beat.

But Papi would put a twenty-dollar bill down, & those dudes
learned quick: shorty had patient fingers & played three moves
      ahead.

Most important, I loved   how much
Papi loved to watch me win.

———

I began competing in chess tournaments
when I was in second grade.

From September to June,
Papi never missed one of my matches.

Never complained about picking me up from
late team meetings or the cost of additional coaching,

even though I knew he must have cut funds
from other places & people to afford both.

Every couple of years
he built a new shelf with his own hands

& put up my trophies & plaques,
pinned up my ribbons & awards.

"Negra bella, lo vas a ganar todo."
& so I did. I won everything for him.

Until I couldn't. Until I didn't know why
or how   I should.

———

Did I love chess?
I did chess.

But love? Like I love
watching beauty tutorials?

Love, like I love when
something I say catches Dre

by surprise & her laugh is Mount Vesuvius—
an eruption that unsettles & shakes

me to my core? Love, like I love the scent
of Mami cooking mangú & frying salami?

Or how I love Papi's brother, Tío Jorge,
holding my hand & saying I make him proud

for myself not for what I win?

Like I loved my father, that kind of love?
Consuming, huge, a love that takes the wheel,

a love where I pretended to be something I wasn't?
I *did* chess. I was obsessed with winning.

But never love.

———

Mami wanted me to be a lady:
sit up straight, cross my ankles,

let men protect me.
Papi wanted me to be a leader.

To think quick & strike hard,
to speak rarely, but when I did,

to always be heard. Me?
Playing chess taught me a queen is both:

deadly & graceful, poised & ruthless.
Quiet & cunning. A queen

offers her hand to be kissed,

& can form it into a fist
while smiling the whole damn time.

But what happens when those principles
only apply in a game? & in the real world,

I am not treated as a lady or a queen,
as a defender or opponent

but as a girl so many want to strike off the board.

———

I've always wanted to go to the Dominican Republic.
Every year my father left on his trip.

Every year I asked if I could go along.
But Papi always said no. I assumed

it was because he was busy with work.
I never thought Papi would be doing

something he didn't want me to see.
Mami's straight up told me since I was five

she wouldn't let me set foot on the island
if it was the last inhabitable place on earth.

Although she still has cousins there,
she hasn't been back once.

I assumed Mami had bad memories of home.
Clearly, I made a lot of assumptions.

I've always looked at my parents & seen
exactly what they've shown me. I could not

imagine them as real humans
who lied. & kept the truth. From each other.

From me.
This year, I did not ask.

I did not want to sit across from my father.
Not to play chess, not to share a meal.

Not to ask if I could join him
on a trip to the Caribbean

when I already knew
way more than I should

about the answer he would give me,
about the answers he would not.

———

I was raised so damn Dominican.
Spanish my first language,

bachata a reminder of the power of my body,
plátano & salami for years before I ever tasted

peanut butter & jelly sandwiches.
If you asked me what I was,

& you meant in terms of culture,
I'd say Dominican.

No hesitation,
no question about it.

Can you be from a place
you have never been?

You can find the island stamped all over me,
but what would the island find if I was there?

Can you claim a home that does not know you,
much less claim *you* as its own?

———

CAMINO ✈ YAHAIRA

Five Days After

Papi had stubby fingers with the tip of one missing
from where a machete slipped one July day
while he was cutting me a mango in the backyard.

His skin where the nail used to be is the same dark color
as the mahogany chess pieces he played with.
(He tried to teach me the game

but I kept trying to include my Barbies in the battle.)

People barely noticed the missing fingertip,
until you shook—in my case, held—his hand & could feel
the shortened pointer finger.

Not that he tried to hide it. Papi wore his fat gold rings
& gestured with every word he said.
& held a cigar to his mouth with the missing finger pointing
    upward.

It's just the rest of him took up a whole room
& it was hard to notice he had anything missing at all
except when he was the one missing,

& then it was like days were deflated,
like when his flight rose into the sky
he took all the air on earth with him.

———

No hay sobrevivientes.
No hay sobrevivientes.
There are no survivors.

It was a foolish hope.

Tía hugs me to her,
her white head wrap caressing my cheek.
She is a small woman & I tower over her.

Neighbors pour into the house
like our grief is a bottomless thirst
& God has tipped this pitcher of people to fill us up.

The furniture is pushed back & an Hora Santa begins.
Rosary beads pass through fingers, & the rosario repeats &
    repeats.
Dios te salve, María, llena eres de gracias.

Fifty Ave Marias, five Padre Nuestros, five Gloria al Padres.
Tía shoves her words out; I repeat them,
rocking back & forth, let the words wash over me.

Later, Tía will hold a private prayer in her bóveda out back;
this is where she keeps her cowrie shells, where she will divine
from the Saints the next steps we should take;

they know all about folks crossing the Atlantic & not surviving.

We stack our faith up like spinal discs to hold us upright;
it gives us language to fill our mouths & hearts & ears.
Gives us deities to call on

that might answer & bring my father home.

———

Papi knew my mother since they were children.
Grew up right here, in this neighborhood of Sosúa.
They were of this home, of each other.

Grew up   grew apart
at least that is what Tía says, that she remembers
how her little sister made eyes at the boy across the way.

They reconnected one day at El Malecón.
She was sitting near the water, gossiping
with a friend from university.

Mamá saw him approaching & fluffed her hair.
Papi straightened his collar. Tucked his shirt in tighter.
She laughed when her friend stuck out her hand, preened.

Papi looked taken aback.
She watched as her friend flaunted & flirted.
Papi gave Mamá a smile & secret wink.

She watched Papi extract his hand from her friend's.
Papi extended it to Mama.
She said he had his heart in it.

Although the friend was clearly taken by him,
Mamá said he had eyes for only her.
Said that at the meeting she knew he'd be

the greatest love of her life.

The day Mamá took to the fever,
Tía was paying house calls to others
who'd been struck by the dengue.

It was just me & Mamá at home
as I wiped her forehead & prayed.
When Tía got home she hopped on the phone,

& even as a kid I knew she was calling
my father. For all her remedies, there are times
when Tía knows a hospital is best.

Mamá did not want to go. Said an ambulance was too expensive.
Although Don Mateo offered his car,
Mama was worried about getting him sick.

She said we were making a big fuss,
even though she could barely speak.
It didn't help that Papi's money came too late.

Mamá died two days later.
It is not something I talk about.
Almost a decade after her passing.

Tía had always lived with us
& she mothered me the best she could.
Some folks would resent this.

But even when Mamá was alive,
Tía was the other
mother of my heart.

The one who would sing to me
when I fell & bumped my butt:
Sana, sana, culito de rana.

When he visited, Papi would tell me stories of Mamá.
How beautiful she was, brown-skinned & petite.
How hardworking she was as a maid at the resort.

He would tell me of their first date,
& the song that reminds him most of her.
My head fills with memories not my own, that paint her for me.

I've never once felt orphaned.
Not with Tía dogging my steps & smacking my hand,
& wiping my tears & telling me what my mother would say.

Not even though Papi was far,
because his presence filled the house:
his weekly phone calls & video chats,

his visits in the summer making Christmas
feel like a semiannual event.
I never felt like an orphan until today.

Two months to seventeen, two dead parents,
& an aunt   who looks worried
because we both know, without my father

without his help   life as we've known it has ended.

———➤———

Carline texts me & I know she's still at work.
The resort is the only place where she has access to Wi-Fi.
She asks me how I'm doing, but I barely reply.

I must have sounded unconvincing when I told her I was fine,
because she arrives at my house after nine,
her feet swollen & shuffling, the tired bagging under her eyes.

She is still gorgeous. & I tell her so.

"Ay, Camino. No me tires piropos.
I know I look exhausted. This li'l one kept me
up all night playing volleyball in my belly.

& the manager ran me ragged today."

It is a good job that Papi helped her get
when she found out half a year ago she was pregnant
& stopped going to school two towns over.

I want to tell her she needs to slow down on hours,
but everyone in her family has to work. It's how they eat.
Her boyfriend, Nelson, contributes best he can,

taking night classes & working two jobs even though he's only
      nineteen.
Tía places some fried fish in front of Carline,
who expertly pulls the flesh,

leaving the sharp-boned carcass completely clean.

When she is done she puts her feet up, & I stand behind her
weaving her hair into braids. So much has changed:
a year ago we would have sat just like this, whispering

about boys & dreams, & what we could be.
Now both of us are moving moment to moment.
Carline came to offer comfort, but I end up being the one

who wraps a blanket around her when she dozes off,
finishes doing her hair gently so she can sleep in
in the morning, parents her as best I can

before she becomes one. & I remember I have none.

—————●—————

Ten Days After

I keep going to school as if nothing's happened.
There was one day where we had one moment of silence.
Most of the kids know I had a father in the States who sends
    money.

I am an oddity at the school.
Never been an hija de mami y papi,
children of white-collared, white-colored society types.

The rich, light-skinned Dominicans at this school
come from families who own factories
or are children of American diplomats.

I didn't have a quinceañera at a country club.
I'm American-adjacent. With a father who makes—made—
enough money to keep me in the school uniform

but not enough to contribute to the annual
fundraiser or to send me on any of the international trips
or to give me a brand-new car over Christmas break.

Papi paid just enough for tuition every quarter,
& sometimes I had to nag him when he forgot
& I'd gotten yet another payment-notification letter.

& now, I sit silently in class. Do not raise my hand.

I've been doing my assignments late at night
after Tía falls asleep. I've been studying for final exams
on the bus ride to school in the morning.

I am pretending Papi being dead does not change anything.
That submitting all my work means my plans will come true.
Even as I sit at a desk I know I may not return to in the fall.

Dreams are like the pieces of fluff that get caught in your hair;
they stand out for a moment, but eventually you wash them
away, or long fingers reach in & pluck them out

& you appear as what everyone expects.

———

I come from people
who are no longer alive.
My grandparents,

my parents. I have
Tía, & my father's brother,
who lives in New York,

& they are the only two
left to me who share my blood.
There is no one to go live with.

There is no one to provide help.
There are my good grades
& my aunt's aging hands.

When I am called to
the guidance counselor,
who wants to know

if I am doing okay,
I ask if she knows what will happen
if my family cannot pay tuition.

She says there are scholarships
I would have had to apply to
a semester ago;

she says funds have been allocated.
But if worse came to worst
they would figure things out

& readmit me next spring semester.
She says she wants me to succeed,
it might just take time to figure things out.

She says this with a small apologetic smile.

It would delay my graduation,
it would delay my ability to apply to college,
& it would delay just how much time

I live here.

———

On her next day off, Carline
drags me out of the house.
We do not turn to the beach

but instead walk over a mile
to a small strip of stores
where the tourists buy bathing suits

& faceless dolls & seashell souvenirs.
Although her breathing is heavy & her feet
are swollen, she says she needed fresh air.

But I know she means *I* needed a change.
Carline would have been a great doctor or nurse.
She has a sharp eye & was good at science.

We gaze into window after window,
pretending to be high-class ladies
who would wear fancy cover-ups over our bathing suits

& flip-flops that cost enough to cover our tabs at el colmado.
I only let Carline walk a bit more before I steer her to an
    ice-cream shop.
She won't ever complain about her aches,

but I know the signs of fatigue.
I only have a few pesos to my name
but I plan to use a handful to buy us each a scoop.

The lady at the counter takes one look at Carline
& then another look at me & waves my little coins away.
She even adds extra sprinkles with her wink.

Her gesture makes me want to cry. The kindness
of a stranger, simply because she sees in us
something worthy of this small gift.

This everyday kindness in my home.
Even if I could leave,
how would I stomach it?

The thought curdles, sour as bad milk.

———

Carline & I walk back home arm in arm.
Our ice-cream-sticky fingers making me feel six years old again.
This day feels like a hundred other days we've spent just like this.

Looking into windows & imagining a different life
with each other by our sides.
Papi put me in the International School after Mamá's death.

But Carline & I remained friends outside of school.
Tía would leave me at her house when she had errands;
Carline's maman would send her to stay with us

when her parents took trips back to Haiti.
& so we know the different kinds of stories
our silence can tell.

Her silence tells me: Camino. I'm scared. This baby is coming.
Camino. I hate my job. Where the manager pinches my butt
& I have to smile when I feel like crying.

My silence tells her: Carline. I know. I know. I know.
Where do we go? Where is safe harbor? Together
can we swim there? Can we carry our families on our backs?

For just a moment   I grab my worries by the nape.

My silence tells them: Leave me. Leave me.
Leave me alone. We will make it. We will be fine.
I promise. Some way   we'll survive.

———

CAMINO ✈ YAHAIRA

Fourteen Days After

My school absences are not a secret.

I've been skipping school on & off for two weeks.
& when I go back, somehow we are taking finals.

I let my teachers' words float around me
but have no idea what is due when or to who.

It all feels like such a fake world.
None of this can be real. How is it almost summer break?

What does an essay on *The Tempest* matter?
What does an analysis of the Hoover presidency matter?

What does an exam in trigonometry matter?
Which one of those things will explain mechanical failure?

Which one of those things will ease how difficult it feels to
    breathe?
I stare out the windows into the warm mid-June day.

Papi left every year

                    from June until September.

Maybe the only way to make it through these days
is to pretend that in the fall he'll be coming back.

———

I am not the only one
skipping responsibilities.

Ma has not been to work
in two weeks, & last night

the spa owner called the house phone
& left a voice mail.

Today, I wake Ma up,
brush her hair into a ponytail.

I clear the chipped polish
off her nails & swipe on a pretty pink color.

I force her into a black dress
that fits much looser than it used to.

I hand her her purse
& order her a Lyft.

"Go, Ma. You have to
do something to take

your mind off of it all.
No one does your job better than you."

She gets in the car
but shakes her head sadly.

My mother, always so organized
& ready, the general

of the small spa she manages,
looks lost & tense.

I watch the car until
it turns the corner

& hold back the impulse
to chase after it,

to call Ma & ask her
to come back. To not leave.

To never leave.

———•———

I'm used to clocks. To using time to succeed.
To slapping my palm hard across a timer

as if it were running its smart mouth.
You don't have to be God to control time.

To learn speed. They say the plane
went down too fast. For life vests. Or safety plans.

Too perpendicular to readjust   in time.
For a rescue to be mounted. By the time the Coast

Guard reached the sinking tail, they'd been under water
for hours. The impact alone would have killed them.

No one ever emerged. The doors never opened.
The air masks never even dropped down.

Without fail, most days I'm in school,
I get sent to the guidance counselor.

But I don't have anything to tell her.
She asks me how I'm doing. Stupid fucking question.

I want to tell her some days I wake up
to find dents on the inside of my palms

from where I've fisted my hands while sleeping,
my nails biting into the skin & leaving angry marks.

On the days I wake up with smooth palms I'm angry at myself.
There should be no breaks from this grief. Not even in sleep.

I don't tell her that. I don't tell her anything.
I chew on the little green mints she offers & wait for the bell.

———

On the days like today that I don't go to school,
I still go over to Dre's house.

Even when she's not there.

Dr. Johnson puts her arm around my shoulders
& tells me to take my time. Her semester ended

a few weeks ago, & she won't teach
a summer session for a few weeks more.

I decide to organize the books in their living room library
while I wait for Dre to come home.

Clear steps: organize the books by genre,
then alphabetize them on the dining room table.

Since they moved here, Dr. Johnson has let me borrow
lots of books. Let me borrow games,

& Wi-Fi, & a cup of sugar if Mami was baking.
& I wish I could borrow time,

or space, or answers. I tell Dr. Johnson this,
& she pat-pats my hand.

"Just let yourself mourn, sweetie.
You can't run from what hurts you,

or like a dog smelling fear,
that grief will just keep chasing with ever-sharp teeth."

I go back to stacking books.
Orderly. Logical. Safe.

———

Later that day, when Ma gets home
I search her face for signs of how she feels.

She is as polished as when she left this morning.
But her face is pale, & her hands tremble

when she hands me her purse. She does not say
how much it must have cost her to smile today.

At six o'clock, Mami & I go to a grief counseling session.
It's the third time the neighborhood association's invited us.

There's a Spanish-speaking counselor & a priest.
Mami grips my hand, her pale cheeks paler.

The room is full. & even before anyone speaks,
there are several people silently weeping.

Pain hums in the room, like a TV on mute,
& there is no knob to turn it off.

The counselor asks us about loss.
I do not know how to say in Spanish:

I am a graceful loser.

Many times. Many things. I've made mistakes
that lost the match.

Who were Mami & I playing against? Did God win?
Did Papi lose? I know we did.

How could the stakes have been so high?
We are sitting in a circle.

One man says both his parents were on the flight;
they were returning to Santo Domingo to retire.

A young woman with straight hair that hangs to her waist
says her husband had just got back from fighting overseas;

he was going to visit his sister
& the place where he was born for the first time in twenty years.

We hear about a little girl going to visit her grandmother,
about a young couple flying to their honeymoon.

The stories hang in the room like twinkling lights
that I could touch. Over 80 percent of the people on the flight

had connections to the island. Returning.
& when it's Mami's turn to talk, in a soft voice she simply says,

"My husband travels back every year.
I feel as if I lose him again   every morning I wake up."

Anger swirls up my chest, gets tangled with the words
I had meant to say. Mami's pain seems hungry.

& for the first time I wonder if now that Papi's dead,
will she learn what I knew? What I haven't been able

to talk to her about for over a year, because I didn't want
her hurt? Because I was afraid of the kind of change

these secrets would rain on our lives.

& if she doesn't find out, does that mean the only person
in my family who knows Papi's secret is me?

When it's my turn to speak, I bite the insides of my cheek.
The only thing I give the circle is a tight smile & shrug.

On silent accord, Mami & I agree, we will not go back.
The emotions at the group session

took up every vacancy in our body
& we have no room   no room   no room left.

———

My old chess coach calls when we get home
after the grief session. I'm doing dishes,

cleaning plates Mami & I filled with food but never ate from.
My hands are soapy when Mami hands me the phone.

Coach Lublin's voice is gentle, soothing;
it's the voice he uses when a newbie

loses a tournament to a kid half their age.
"Yahaira, we are all thinking of you."

Coach & I worked together for two years.
He seemed unsurprised when I quit the chess team,

as if he'd always known I was not truly interested.
He always smiles at me in the hallway

& invites me to drop by training sessions
but has never pressured me to rejoin the team.

When I hear his voice

my heart squeezes, a wrung-out sponge,
& I wonder what will happen to the phone

if I drop it into the filled sink. Will it float on suds
or be weighed down to the bottom?

How does the water learn to readjust around the new object?
Could we nestle the phone in rice, revive it into ringing again?

Mami looks up sharply from the table
& gives me her *look*.

"Thank you, Coach," I say to his kind remarks.
Who knew death must be so damn polite?

———◆———

Our apartment has plastic-covered leather sofas,
windows with frilly curtains;

my mother decorates with wide sashes,
color-coded to match the season.

There's a small courtyard out back
where we held summer barbecues for the family

& neighbors. Unlike most of my friends' families,
Papi & Ma owned our apartment in the co-op.

Bought it when they found out
Mami was pregnant with a girl.

Papi said his queens needed a castle
& Morningside Heights would provide.

More & more, I sit on the fire escape
just to get a chance to breathe.

Our house these days is a choked-up throat.
I cannot exhale myself out the front door.

This is no castle. It's an altar to a man,
a National Geographic shrine;

the house is a living sadness, & as Mami walks
its halls at night, even the floorboards weep.

Fifteen Days After

It's Saturday.
After three p.m.

I lie in bed.
The doorbell rings.

Maybe Mami will get it.
Footsteps coming down the hall.

Soft padding
that doesn't belong

to Tío Jorge or Mami.
Soft murmurs outside my door.

More than one person
came inside.

Mami's quivering voice
& another tone more sure.

My door's pushed open.

I keep my eyes closed.
If they are intruders

I hope they steal everything,
especially the weight on my chest.

I hear sneakers
thump on the ground.

Then a body settles on my bed.
"Move over," Dre says.

She must have come over
with Dr. Johnson,

otherwise she would have ducked
through the window.

I am right; I hear Dr. Johnson's
measured murmur cutting through

my mother's choked voice.

Dre puts her arms around me.
& it's the first time I've let myself be held

since Papi died.

When Dre grabs the bottle of acetone
from on top my dresser I'm surprised.

If it weren't for me, the only decoration
on her nails would be specks of soil.

But it's not her nails she's concerned with.
She takes a little ball of cotton

& begins removing the polish from mine.
Despite having done the same for Mami's nails

yesterday, it's only then I notice,

I've bitten the color off my own.
When both my hands

are clean & she's filed the nails down for me,
I grab her face. Her eyes are calm.

My old-soul girlfriend. Always watching.
Always watching out for me.

We share a breath before I kiss her,
before I bite back the hitch of tears.

———•———

Positive identifications have been made,
& Papi's gold-tooth smile was among them.

Tío Jorge & his wife,
Tía Mabel, show up at 4:05 p.m.

My mother's sister, Tía Lidia,
& my cousin Wilson show up at 4:32.

My father's cousins, who work at the billiards,
show up at 5:12.

The family comes with food, with Bibles,
with worry sewn into the creases of their foreheads.

There is no music playing.

The men talk quietly in the living room
& sip Johnnie Walker.

When Tía Lidia & Mami go to her room to pray,
Tía Mabel appoints herself the general of logistics,

doing the things that Ma has been unable
or unwilling to do.

She calls a cousin about flowers,
a childhood neighbor about casket costs.

She calls a church a few blocks away
to have his name read at morning mass for a week.

She calls a relative in the Dominican Republic,
is quiet a long time while someone on the other end speaks.

There is a call made to *El Diario* newspaper
about publishing an obituary.

My cousin Wilson sits on hold with the airline,
trying to see when we can claim what is left.

The other women come back from the bedroom.
Mami's eyes are dry & hard.

Discussion turns to burial plots
& whether or not the remains should be taken to DR.

My father was the one who always threw the get-togethers
& even in death, he brings us all home.

———

Tío Jorge breaks away from the men
when he sees me standing

in the living room doorway,
swaying on my feet.

He leads me to my father's favorite chair,
awkwardly pats back my hair. I curl into his hand.

Tío Jorge & Tía Mabel do not have children
but they would have made great parents.

Tío Jorge knows how to listen.
Even if all he hears is silence.

We sit like that a long while.
Him patting my hair, me breathing in

his familiar cologne.
                                    I trust he hurts

how I hurt. I trust he knows I hurt
without my having to say so.

Halfway through the discussion
of funeral arrangements

I heave up from Papi's chair.
Walk to his old-school record player,

grab one of his favorite artists,
& queue the music.

My uncles go quiet,
my aunt shushes someone on the phone,

I lean back in his chair
& close my eyes.

One of Papi's favorite bachata songs
lifts itself into the room. It's about lost love,

& although it's a breakup song,
the lament to not think, to not cry,

to not hurt for another man   the singer
feels like it could be speaking to this moment.

Before the song is over
Mami slams her hand on the disc.

The music stops midnote.

It seems fitting, I think.
To end right in the middle.

She doesn't have to tell me
music is inappropriate for mourning.

I only needed it for a second
to remember a time before this one.

———

Tía Mabel
asks Mami

where Papi
will be buried

as we're seated
around the kitchen table

picking out
a picture

to laminate
for mourners.

———

(I have begun making lists in my head.
Of all the things I don't want to forget about Papi.

If someone asked my biggest fear,
it would be that. Forgetting his calloused hand

with a fingertip he chopped off in DR.
His gold tooth that blinked in the light.

His big laugh that used to make me smile,
even if I was mad at him.

I try to find a picture that captures all of this,
Papi in motion. Papi in space. Papi gilded.

Papi, the big hot boiling sun
we all looked to for light.

I want to forget this whole past year
& remember only the good things.

Not a single photo captures exactly what I need,
& I shove away picture after picture after picture—)

———

At Tía's words

Something flashes in Mami's eyes that isn't really sadness;
her hands tighten against her snatched waist.

She hugs herself hard. Neither of them looks at me when she
    says:
"His real family is here. What's left of him will be buried here."

I look at my mother, as if seeing her for the first time.
She sounds angry. I try to see if she knows what I know.

But Tía Mabel makes a sharp sound,
& I swing my eyes in her direction.

Tía Mabel's mouth looks like a cliff words want to tumble over,
but she clamps her lips tight & pulls the sentences off the edge.

Tío Jorge shakes his head.
"Yano always wanted to be buried back home, Zoila."

Mami doesn't even look in his direction.
"He will not be buried there. I am his wife."

My heart feels like it's pounding in my chest.
Does she know? Does she know? Do they all know?

Tío shakes his head & takes a folder out from his briefcase.
"His wife you might be, Zoila, but you are not his will."

He sets a document on the kitchen table.
My mother picks up the papers

as if they will origami themselves into fangs.
Then she laughs, "So *this* he planned for?"

"& . . ." Tío shoots a glance at me.
"The other matter, too, Zoila. You agreed."

Mami puts the papers down without reading,
straightens & smooths them as if fixing a boyfriend's tie.

Mami turns her back to us, stands by the window.
"He was ours first. & he will be ours last.

Pero if this is what he wanted, then take him back.
But we won't be the ones there to see him buried."

———

I want to agree with Mami, but I can't.
The part of me that is my father's daughter,

that sat on his lap & laughed. That had her hand
patiently guided by his, that girl knows it isn't so simple.

"If Papi is buried in DR, I want to be there.

He died alone & afraid, without family around.
Without anyone who knew him. He was probably thinking of us.

How can we put him in the dirt alone
& not even go to say a prayer over his grave?"

Although she still has her back to me, Mami straightens.

The longer I speak, the more unthinkable the scenario.
Mami can't possibly imagine she & I wouldn't go.

Papi wasn't perfect, but he didn't deserve this.
& we deserve to say goodbye.

Her eyes are watery when she turns to me,
but her voice is solid ice.

"Yahaira. Your father was no man's saint.
Not even if I dropped dead this moment, would I let you

touch foot on the sands of that tierra. Get that thought
right out of your head. Grave or no grave."

I press my mouth tight to keep my quivering lip to myself.
& I look at my mother & smile.

                    Never, ever let anyone see you sweat.
& if my mother paid attention

at a single one of my matches
she knows: when Yahaira Rios smiles

just before she makes a move,
you better watch the fuck out.

———

Mami, is a good woman, a good woman.
Mami is smart & shows up to school conferences,

Mami is a good woman, a good woman.
she works hard & always makes dinner.

Mami is a good woman, a good woman.
She never forgot to pick me up from school,

Mami is a good woman, a good woman.
she sewed my sweaters when I pulled a button,

Mami is a good woman, a good woman,
mended the holes I tore in my new jeans.

Mami is a good woman, a good woman,
she buys thoughtful presents & kisses loudly,

Mami is a good woman, a good woman,
& I know I failed her.

———

Mami wanted a girl
she could raise in her own image, & I came forth

a good girl, a good girl, but so much of me
when I was younger seems crafted

from my father's spit, as if he shone

a light on her womb & pressed a fingerprint
onto my forehead, baptized me his alone;

I have words that I have kept secret from Mami,
words a better daughter would have said.

I am my father's daughter, a bad daughter,
a bad daughter to a great woman.

———

The thing I learned
about my father

is like a smudge
on an all-white dress.

You hope if you don't
look at it, if you

don't rub your finger
in the spot   then maybe

it won't spread. Then maybe
it will be unnoticed.

But it's always there.
A glaring fault.

———

Papi had another wife.
I found the marriage certificate.

The date on the form
was a few months after

my parents' own marriage
here in the States.

& as if to ensure
that anyone who stumbled

across this envelope
got it right, there was also

a small picture included. My father
with a beautiful brown woman

with long dark hair,
both of them in all white

as she carried a bouquet,
smiling up into his face

while he stared steadily
& seriously at the camera.

My father had another wife,
& I know my mother

could not have known.
Could not have been the type

to stay, while her husband strayed
year after year after year.

This other woman,
the reason my father left me,

left us   broke trust   ignored
the family he left behind.

& when he returned last summer,

I didn't know how to look
him in the face & pretend.

So it was easier not to look at him at all.
When the only words I owned

were full of venom, it seemed better
to stop speaking to this man

since the only option was to poison us all.

———◆———

CAMINO ✈ YAHAIRA

Nineteen Days After

I haven't talked to El Cero since he last approached me,
but today, as I'm squeezing the water from my hair,
he comes out from behind the trees.

Vira Lata was chewing on some bones as I left the house
& didn't join me on this trip to the water,
but still I scan the tree line hoping to see him napping in the
     shade.

A small patch of short curly hair springs up
from the neck of El Cero's shirt. I am reminded
he might smile boyishly, but he is not a boy.

I am glad I am near home,
that there are houses beyond the clearing.
Because in this moment, I am a girl a man stares at:

I am not a mourning girl. I am not a grieving girl.
I am not a parentless girl. I am not a girl without means.
I am not an aunt's charity case. I am not almost-alone.

None of those things matter.

He approaches, wide-mouth smiling.
"I have my motorbike." He points. "Want a ride home?"
He wraps his hand around my wrist.

———

I snatch my arm away as my
cell phone starts ringing.
I scramble to grab the phone from my back pocket.

Tía's name flashes on the screen.
"¿Aló, Tía?" I back away from El Cero.
Tía does not say one word

but I hear the tears in her sharp breaths.

"They found him. I just got word that four days ago
they found what is left of him.
& they have decided to bring him home."

I murmur to Tía but know she cannot hear me.
A body means there is no miracle to hope for;
dead is dead is dead. For four days I didn't know.

You did know, I tell myself.
We knew there were no survivors.
But somehow this proof sledgehammers my heart.

Someone needs to light the candles,
to call the funeral home & contact his friends.
Someone needs to make flower arrangements & call a church.

& the only someone is me. I put the phone in my back pocket.
Confronting El Cero face-to-face. "Whatever you want from me,
forget it. I have nothing to give you."

It makes me sick that I find out this news
here, in this place I love, with a man
I am growing to hate.

I rush away from him, but not before I hear him say:
"But, Camino, you owe me more than you think,
& hasn't it always been about what I can offer you?"

———

When I get home, Tía has lit candles.
Although he was not her brother,
I can't imagine what she must feel.

I've known my father my whole life.
She knew my father all of his.
Tía was a healer's apprentice as a child,

seven years old, and in the room when Papi was born,
years later saw him fall in love with my mother.
She was the first person to hold his child.

Even when he came to visit
this house he paid for & updated,
Papi treated Tía like an older sister:

so much respect for how she kept the house,
for the beliefs she had,
the decisions she made regarding my well-being.

They were friends. But until this moment
I have not thought of what she's lost.
He was like her brother. Besides me, her only family.

& on this day   that ends all hope
we hold each other close   thinking of a man
& all the people that must live on without him.

———

Tía tells me she has heard rumors.
She is speaking to me the next morning
as we await news regarding Papi's body.

Her hands pluck the feathers off a chicken.
She is methodical, her fingers fast along the fluff
that she drops into a plastic bag in the kitchen sink.

The big machete that is never far from her side
catches the light through the window; it glints at me
& I wish I could carry it with me.

Tía tells me both Don Mateo & the woman who sells fruit
have mentioned seeing El Cero waiting for me after school,
or walking from the beach soon after I've left it.

She says the Saints have whispered caution in her ear.
I take a deep breath; I want to tell Tía it's all true.
That I'm afraid of the thing El Cero wants to ask of me.

Her voice is stripped of any emotions.
But if fingers can be angry,
hers must be wrathful; she plucks in hard snatches.

"I raised you smart. Right, girl?"
This is not a question she actually wants answered.
I can tell by how fast she speaks.

Tía's anger now sounds like it could be directed at me.
That thought puts a staying hand
on the words that were going to leap from my lips.

"I raised you clean & fed,
even when my feet were soiled,
when my own stomach rumbled. Right, girl?

I grew you up for a future
different than the one most girls
around here are allowed.

Choices. Did I not do everything
to provide you choices?"
The feathers bulge in the bag,

& I wish I was just as light.
But I feel weighed down,
her words turned to stones.

Tía thinks I have been inviting El Cero's attention.
Somehow his stalking has turned into
something I must have done.

The chicken is nearly naked.

Raw & puckered, dressed in saggy skin.
A feast for our hunger,
a place to gnash our teeth

since neither one of us can bite at the world.

———

I wish I could tell Tía
that El Cero won't leave me alone.
I haven't done anything wrong

or encouraged him in any way.
He just shows up, grinning,
waiting.

   I wish I could tell Tía
I don't know what to do. That
I'm scared he'll corner me.

     I wish
I could tell Tía, but what would
Tía do if she knew? Tía is older,

   with little money. She is
respected in the neighborhood
& beloved by the people to whom

she offers care, but El Cero occupies
a world of men who care little of healers,
& even less of the girls

who represent little more than dollar signs.
Don Mateo is old. Tío Jorge does not know me.
There is no one to stop El Cero. Anymore.

What would El Cero do to Tía
if she tried to stand up to him?
I cannot even think the thought.

———

I am from a playground place.
Our oceans   that we need for fish
are cleared so extranjeros can kite surf.

Our land, lush & green, is bought
& sold to foreign powers so they can build
luxury hotels for others to rest their heads.

The bananas & yucca & sugarcane
farmed & harvested, exported,
while kids thank God for every little scrap.

The developed world wastes gas,
raises carbon emissions & water levels
that threaten to disappear us in a single gulp.

Even the women, girls like me,
our mothers & tías, our bodies
are branded jungle gyms.

Men with accents pick us
as if from a brochure to climb
& slide & swing. & him?

El Cero? He has his hand in every pocket.

If you are not from an island,
you cannot understand
what it means to be of water:

to learn to curve around the bend,
to learn to rise with rain,
to learn to quench an outside thirst

while all the while
you grow shallow
until there is not one drop

left for you.

I know this is what Tía does not say.
Sand & soil & sinew & smiles:
all bartered. & who reaps? Who eats?

Not us. Not me.

———

Tía doesn't believe girls should wear all black.
I was thirteen the first time she let me buy a black dress
I wanted for my middle school graduation.

It's this same black dress I pull out from the closet
to wear to the meeting with the priest.
It still fits. I slide on the straps.

I pull on black stockings despite the heat outside.
Tía doesn't blink when she sees me.
She just turns around so I can button her white blouse.

She wears a white head wrap too.
I know the priest will raise a brow, but Tía doesn't care.
She is armored in her Saints,

& they make her brave, or reckless, or are they the same?
All white like this shows undue devotion to the Saints,
& our priests don't want to know what's practiced in secret.

Tía & I stare at the mirror. The two of us framed in copper.
Tears pool in her gaze & I immediately wipe them
where they collect in the wrinkles around her eyes.

She doesn't flinch at my hand. She curls into my palm.
Tía doesn't believe girls should wear black.
But if I wasn't a woman before today,

I think I am one now.

When I ask Tía
if my father's brother, Tío Jorge,
will be coming with Papi's body,

she hesitates a long moment
& fingers a loose fringe
that's fallen free from her head wrap.

"Bueno, te digo que no sé."
But her tense shoulders
seem to know more

than she's telling me.
I look at her sideways
& we walk arm in arm into the church.

"How are we to plan a funeral
if we don't know who's coming?
Will people be staying with us?

How much do we need to cook?"
A hundred other questions puff into dandelions,
wisp up in the air between us

but Tía just shakes her head
& doesn't make a wish
on a single one.

In the middle of the night,
 Tía shakes me awake from a dream
  where I am wandering New York City

screaming my father's name.
 At first, I think I must have been screaming out loud,
  but when my eyes adjust to the dark

I see Tía is carrying her healer's bag.
 I get dressed quickly in jeans & sandals.
  Do not bother putting on a bra, or brushing my hair.

I can tell by the worried way she rifles inside her bag
 that this is an emergency situation.
  As if we don't have enough to deal with.

When we step outside the house, a young man waits.
 Shadows darken his face, but as I get closer,
  I see it's Nelson, Carline's boyfriend,

who made eyes at her since she was five
 & we would all splash each other in the ocean
  like we'd discovered a personal water park.

He must have been recruited to fetch us.
 I do not ask what is wrong. There is only one reason.
  We walk the uneven streets in the dark,

Tía's white clothing a splash of brightness against the unlit night.
        Good thing we know this ramshackle neighborhood
                as well as we know the webs between our fingers.

She stops in front of the yellow house,
        & there must be a power outage
                because inside is pitch black

except for a couple of candles burning in the window.
        Carline's maman opens the door.
                Although it is dark, I can see the one-room house

is swept clean & scrubbed cleaner.
        But still too small for all the people
                we must fit inside:

Maman & Carline's father,
        an older man who rarely smiles,
                & Tía & myself, & Nelson.

& Carline. & Carline's babe   attempting to push itself out.
        Carline's face is red & sweaty; she is sprawled
                on a faded couch, her hands clutching her belly.

———

I towel off Carline's forehead.
Tía asks Carline's Maman questions
in her calm curandera voice;

"When did the contractions start?"
"When was the last time she went to the clinic?"
"Has her water broken? How long ago?"

Carline clutches my hand tightly,
& I attempt to circle out her worries with my thumb.
If there is anything to be done, Tía will do it.

Carline should be in a hospital,
but Maman says the babe is coming too fast,
& they panicked thinking of the logistics.

It is not an easy thing to do,
for a Haitian parent to bring their child
to a Dominican hospital to give birth.

There is already a lot of tension around
who here deserves care; I cannot fault Maman
for being too afraid.

Tía's questions are asked as firmly as the hand
she presses onto Carline's belly; as a curandera,
Tía is fierce, channeling something beyond herself.

I unfold long white sheets & wrap them around cushions
to protect the space where Carline will give birth.
I use the flashlight on my phone to get my bearings in the house.

Tía pulls her up by the elbows & bears Carline's weight,

then prays & calls protective spirits into the room;
I reach into her bag & grab the tea made from thyme;
Carline's father looks stern, but I see his hands tremble

as he settles them on the back of a chair.
He mumbles under his breath in Kreyòl,
& I wonder if he too is praying.

Tía settles Carline more comfortably
on the birthing bed I've made. She guides Carline to breathe,
to push, to wait. I set thick towels on the floor.

Nelson rushes to help me;
his fingers jerk sharply as we straighten the space.
Fear clouds the room, a thick fog,

but Tía's calm voice is a flame cutting through it.
I switch places with Tía, & my arms grow heavy
where I sit behind Carline, holding her up;

I am sweating almost as hard as she is.
I try to breathe deeply as I hold my best friend up.
I try not to think of all the ways I know premature labor can go
      wrong.

Tía is red in the face & her eyes are weary,
although you can't tell by her steady movements.
"One last hard push, niña, the baby is crowning."

Carline doesn't seem to have any more energy.
She is panting hard, her eyes squeezed shut,
& I am worried if this is not the last push—

"Come now, Carline," I whisper.
"You did not carry this baby all these months,
not to see it into the light. Con fuerza!"

I wipe the sweaty hair at her forehead,
& she weeps into the crook of my arm,
but she pushes. & pushes. & pushes:

      the small body plops down into Tía's waiting hands
          like a wrinkled fruit from a shaken tree.
              The baby boy is tiny. Quiet.

Tía is a woman woven of miracles;
the reason people who are afraid of her
& her magic   still call for the worst emergencies

is because Tiá's a woman who speaks to the dead,
who negotiates with spirits, who loosens their fingers
when they clutch around the neck of someone she wants to
    live—

It doesn't always work—I know personally
sometimes Tía is too late; sometimes the request is too great
& Tía's bargaining not enough; sometimes

Tía is only a healer woman with calloused hands,
a commanding voice, with ointments & tea,
this woman who holds a baby not her own,

says, "Ven   mi'jo   ven."

———◆———

Sometimes, Tía is more:

she calls forward his life when it would retreat,
& the room holds its breath as if we can gift it to the child.
& Carline weeps, & Tía prays & curses & coaxes

a child to breathe breathe breathe
pressing her two fingers against his chest
beating his heart for him   oblivious

to the slick of his body & blue of his lips
to the collective sob of the room
to the spirits who would greet him on their side of the veil.

Tía takes air into her mouth
& pushes it into the child's mouth:
does this again & again

from her body to his   until it seems impossible
this bringing forth of life
when death is so steadily stalking into the room

& then the baby inhales   a deep gasp

          just as the electricity returns to the barrio

               & the small house becomes filled, brilliant bright.

———◆———

I have been so entrenched
in death, & drowning, & funerals,
that this seems an amazing thing

to see this babe clutch at the air.
To see this child who should not be here
not only here but   *here.*

Through my own tears, I see all of us are crying.
& tired Carline holds the child close
to her breasts & grips my hand.

Tía gives instructions of herb teas to brew,
ointments to make, & advice on latching.
She'll come back if Carline needs help swaddling.

Maman hugs me to her chest as we are leaving;
she says thank you & thrusts some pesos at me.
She says she will wash the sheets & return them.

Carline holds her child; Nelson holds his hat.
The old man does not say a word,
but tears trail down his cheeks as he walks us to the door.

———•———

CAMINO ✈ YAHAIRA

They've made a memorial
outside of Papi's billiards.

Under the green lights,
where the bouncers stand,

there's a blown-up picture
of Papi smiling,

holding a glass (of what I imagine
is whiskey) out to the camera.

Dre insisted on coming with me,
& she is a sure presence behind me.

I kneel & touch my hand
to the gifts people left in Papi's honor:

flower wreaths, so many flowers,
although Papi always said

"Why pay money
for a thing that will die in a week?"

The knickknacks build a lump
the size of a billiard cube inside my throat:

A lottery ticket,
a bottle of shoeshine polish,

a small Dominican flag,
a baseball card of Robinson Canó,

a little figurine
of a man dressed in red & black.

In history we learned
the Greeks made sure to die

with a coin in their pocket
to ensure their spirit could pay

for their way to the other side;
remembering this, I give Papi

the only kind of safe passage I have to offer.
I kneel on the cold, hard concrete

& fish the chess piece from my pocket.
Set her, the polished black piece,

right by a burning candle:
a queen to guard him on his way.

Papi's billiards has always been
a gathering place, & as I stand outside of it

I remember my last time here. It was after a match;
Papi took me to his pool hall to celebrate.

He rarely did that, said billiards
wasn't a place for children, especially not his child.

But on this night he wanted to show off
my trophy to his employees & friends.

Surprised me with a cake & a glass of Coke
he had splashed with a little bit of rum.

He pressed a code into the jukebox
so that bachata songs blared out for free all night.

My father left the country a few weeks later.
I stopped playing chess soon after.

———

I am quiet on the train ride home.
My head against Dre's shoulder

as her breath puffs softly into my hair.
She knows I hate riding the train alone;

it's one of the reasons I think
she pressed to come with me tonight.

The last time I played chess
I won, against a boy named Manny

who I'd played against before—
he always smiled at me across the table,

held my hand too long when we shook
& took both his wins & losses gracefully—

but this is not a story about Manny;
this is a story about winning,

about feeling on top of the world,
of feeling like a star had risen inside me

& maybe was shining on my face
or glittering off my trophy last summer

as I stood on the train station platform
& prepared to go home.

Papi was in DR at the time, so I attended the match alone.
It was daytime & the train was packed

& I got on with my back to a man
who leaned against the train doors—

———

& when I felt a squeeze on my leg
I thought it was an accident & when I felt fingers

float up my thighs I thought I must be mistaken
& when he palmed me under my skirt openhanded

I dropped my trophy   but did not scream,
did not make a scene   did not curse him out

there was no strategy   no alternate plan
no way to win, there was just me   stuck,

& being felt up on a public train   racing
northbound   heart   breath

sick   lost   anger has no place on the board
I was impotent in my feeling   never let them

see you sweat   dripped on my brow

I don't think   I liked it. It lasted more than one stop
more than two   more than three

do you know what I mean
my body   was not my body   could not

be mine   he got off at Ninety-Sixth Street
I did not pick my trophy off the train floor   I did not cry

until I got home   until Dre came in through
the window & saw me trembling & held me

close & did not ask me anything but still knew
still must have known   how she ran the bath

& folded my skirt into the farthest corner
of my closet & we never spoke of it

I did not cry over it again   but I knew
I needed to speak to Papi

I hoped he'd have some words of wisdom,
some response. But when I called he did not answer.

———◆———

Once I unfroze from what happened on the train,
I tried frantically to reach him.

I wanted to speak to the most protective
man in my life; I wanted him to undo it somehow.

I had a match in two days, & I wanted to tell Papi
I didn't want to go. I needed a break.

I don't know why I felt like I needed his permission.
After three days with no reply,

I opened the cabinet where Papi put
all his business papers in a folder.

But the only papers were for the billiards here.
Nothing with a Dominican area code.

Then at the bottom of the cabinet,
half hidden by other files, covered in dust,

was the sealed envelope.
I knew I should put it back.

I knew it wasn't what I was looking for.
But I opened it anyway.

———◆———

After what I found & what happened on the train.

I skipped two tournaments.
Ones that had been difficult to qualify for.

But on the evening of the third tournament.
Papi called me huffing   & puffing.

He'd received an email from the tournament commission.
Disqualifying me from any other summer matches.

When I answered the phone.
Papi did not ask if everything was okay.

I did not ask why he read that email
but none of my texts, replied to none of my phone calls.

He did not let me get a word in.
He didn't ask why I answered with so much anger.

& the truth is   I don't think I would have told.

About the man   & the hand   up my skirt. In my panties.
About the certificate in the file cabinet that made my father a
     liar.

But I'll never know. What I would have said.

Because Papi did not ask.
He only lectured me & told me he was disappointed.

After he hung up. I whispered into the phone.
All the ways that I was disappointed in him.

If Papi wanted my silence.
I vowed that day that he would get it.

When Papi came home.
A few weeks before school began back up.

He ranted & raved to Mami that I had grown stubborn.
He would walk into a room & yell I needed to grow up.

I would simply go into my room.
Or climb through Dre's window.

To escape having to look my father in the face.

———

Twenty-One Days After

It's the last day of school.
I walk through the school hallways

like an alien has crept into my body.
My arms don't work like they used to.

I try to raise them to pick up my report card.
I try to make them pick up a pencil as I sign myself out.

I try to open my locker to remove my books.
I try to keep them from trembling.

But they only shake lightly at my side,
& it's Dre who murmurs & reminds me

I can do this. Keep on breathing, I mean,
when it feels like the littlest thing is too much work.

I guess I keep hoping if I just don't move at all
it'll hurt less when the memory barges into me:

It has been three weeks.
I do not have a father anymore.

———————

Insurance representatives for the airline come to the house.
Tío Jorge & Tía Mabel are already here.

Although Tío Jorge practiced law in the Dominican Republic,
I still think we should have a lawyer who practices here,

but no one listens to me.
The airline representatives open a folder

& list the initial findings from the National Transportation
    Safety Board.
I make sure to memorize the name

of the organization that will investigate what happened.
When the reps are done, they look expectantly at us.

Tío Jorge grabs the report & walks to the kitchen window,
reading in the light of the setting sun. Mami looks at me

& I know she wants me to translate; she didn't catch every word.
"Dinero," I tell her softly. An advance payment, to be exact.

So many dollars they've knotted around my father's life.
"Un medio million," Tío Jorge whispers.

No one else says a word. Mami begins to weep
while drilling a manicured nail into the wooden table

until the sound feels like it's puncturing
my ear, & I put my hand over hers.

———•———

The airline	representatives
say	don't say
grievance.	grieve.
say	don't say
unprecedented.	crash.
say	don't say
mechanical failure.	dead.
say	don't say
pilot error.	dad.
say	don't say
insurance policy.	papi.
say	don't say
advance compensation.	his name.
say	don't say
accident.	sorry.
say	"say
loss.	sorry."

I say:

"Say you're sorry."

———◆———

Things you can buy
with half a million dollars:

a car that looks more
like a space creature than a car.

A designer platinum purse
to carry a small dog. A small dog.

A performance by your favorite
musical artist for your birthday.

A diamond-encrusted
bottle of Dominican rum.

A mansion. A yacht. A hundred
acres of land. Houses, but not homes.

All four years of college
or beautician school & certificate.

Five hundred flights
to the Dominican Republic.

A half million Dollar Store chess sets,
with their accompanying boxes.

A hundred thousand copies
of Shakespeare's *The Tempest*.

Apparently   a father.

———

Money like this

makes me think
of a game show.

& I wish
I could phone a friend

or use a lifeline.
I wish a smiling host

would pat my hand & have me
crowdsource the audience

for answers
on what to guess next.

A half million dollars
is more than my dad

ever made,
more than Mami or I

can begin to understand.

———

Tío Jorge says
we should still sue the airline.

Tío Jorge says
it might take years, but we are due a settlement.

Tío Jorge says
he can handle the finances.

Tío Jorge says
he can sell the billiards.

Tío Jorge says
he can open me a trust fund so the money is saved.

Tío Jorge says
he can hire a financial advisor, or accountant.

Tío Jorge says
we need to set money aside for taxes.

Tío Jorge says
this should help with the funeral expenses.

Tío Jorge says
we shouldn't tell the rest of the family.

Tío Jorge says—

Mami cuts him off:
"Jorge. You were your brother's consentido.

& I appreciate your advice.
But the one who needed it was him,

& you didn't offer it when he was here."
I look from Mami to Tío Jorge

trying to understand what isn't being said.
Did Mami know about the certificate?

Did Tío? Mami must realize how harsh she sounds
because she flattens her hands on her thighs.

"I just . . . what I mean is,
Yahaira & I will figure this out on our own."

I've never heard Mami
be so brisk with Tío Jorge.

Tía Mabel lowers her eyes;
she traces the lines of wood on the kitchen table.

Tío Jorge seals his lips like an envelope
& silently exits the room.

———————

There is a community garden
around the corner

where I know I'll find Dre
if she's not home

or answering her phone.
That is her happy place,

& since she is mine
I walk there & sit on a bench.

I watch her long bent back,
the bright purple cap

pulled over her short hair
as she hums something

I'm assuming
is blaring through her ear pods.

Probably Nina Simone.
Dre loves Ms. Nina.

Will play her when she misses her father.
Will play her when she's angry.

Will play her when we see videos on social media
of another black boy shot   another black girl pulled over

another kid in the Bronx stabbed outside a bodega.
Will play her while painting protest signs;

Dre plays Nina when two girls holding hands are jumped
or a kid who calls themselves them

is made fun of & it goes viral—
                Dre turns to Nina.

Turns up "Mississippi Goddam."
Me? I want to bang my fist. I want to scream

the world apart from the seams.
But Dre? She gets a glint in her eye

like she's imagining she can repot us, all of us, onto a new planet
where we can grow with deep & understanding roots,

where we will rise & flourish into tree houses   &
Nina will rain & Nina will breeze & Nina will be the sunshine;

I must make a noise at my imaginings
because Dre turns around, cocks her head,

pulls out her earbud & places it in my ear.
Goes right back to packing dirt around a bed of basil.

Birds flying high   you know how I feel.

CAMINO ✈ YAHAIRA

Tía is angry whispering over the cordless phone again.
She steps onto the balcón as if the short distance
will stop me from overhearing.

When her call is done I go sit with her.
We rock in unison & don't turn on the porch light
as darkness falls & fireflies flitter over us like incandescent
    halos.

Tía has never lied to me. From the beginning,
any questions I asked she answered.
Whether it was about sex, or boys, healing or the Saints.

I keep rocking next to her. Sometimes words
need time to form; the minutes like slabs
building a ramp out the mouth.

Tonight, Tía hums under her breath.
When she abruptly stops her rocking,
I slow my own chair's rhythm.

The porch floorboards echo a creak,
& it feels like the night is making room
for whatever Tía has to say.

I smack a mosquito against my chest.
My own blood smears on my skin.
I'm surprised I didn't notice the sting.

& yet   I know,
whatever Tía is going to say
may not draw blood,

but I will feel it.

———

Tía says,

"The airline has offered money to preempt lawsuits.
A half-million-dollar advance to be split among dependents.
That was your Tío Jorge on the phone. This is complicated."

Tía says,

"I never wanted to lie to you, mi'ja.
Your father was a complex man.
He had many pieces of himself, & many crossroads."

Tía says,

"There is a girl in New York City, your same age.
Your same features. Your same father.
This girl was born two months after you were."

Tía says,

"Your father married hers before he married yours.
You can apply for money as one of his dependents, but
Zoila, the woman he married, might try to fight your claim."

Tía says,

"She, the wife, has connections at the consulate.
She's made it difficult for your father to request you.
He needed her citizenship papers to help obtain your visa."

Tía says

a lot more words, but I barely hear any of them.

I have a sister. I have a sister. I have a sister.

There is another person besides Tía of my blood in the world.

———

A truth
you did not want
to know

can rot & grow mold
in the pit
of your stomach,

can sour
every taste
you've ever had,

can cast a stench
so bad you forget
you've ever known

a sweet thing.
A truth you did not want
can put a collar around your neck

& lead you into the dark,
the places where all your
monsters live.

There is another girl
on this planet
who is my kin.

My father
lied to me
every day of my life.

I am not alone
but the only family
I have besides Tía

are all strangers to me.
I want to put my fingers
against my sister's cheek.

I want to put my face
in her neck & ask
if she hurts the way I do.

Does she know of me?
Would my father have told her?
Did she share

in his confidences?
While the whole while he lied to me?
Or is she the only one

who would understand
my heart right now?
If I find her

would I find a breathing piece
of myself I had not known
was missing?

———

On Tía's altar, there are all sorts of items.
a shot glass half-full of rum, nine vases of water.
There's a bright bouquet of yellow flowers;

A small cup of fresh coffee on the floor. Surrounding the altar
are photos; a black & white photo of her parents: her father,
the fisherman, & my grandmother,

a washerwoman from west of the island. My mother's
smiling face smiles up from the ground as well. Several
great-aunts & -uncles pose stiffly in formal clothing.

& underneath the white tablecloth
is a stack of bills I've snuck onto the altar.
My school tuition is one. It arrives every June,

& Papi pays it off in July. It's the charge for my first-quarter
schooling so I can attend classes in September.
The pesitos people pay Tía are not enough.

My heart thumps hard.
I press a hand to keep it inside.
How does an overeducated orphan

become an obstetrician
in a place where most girls
her age become pregnant

before tenth grade? But now
money is owed to me.
Tía says it could be mine.

How does a girl—*how do I*—
finish high school,
go to college in the US?

How do I watch
every single one of my dreams
flutter like a ribbon of bubbles

pop pop popping in the air. I don't.

———

"Tía, about the visa & the money,
Papi said my papers were in order."
Tía is cleaning red kidney beans for a moro.

She nods but does not say anything.

"Would I still be able to go to the States?
Tío Jorge could take me in, right?"
Tía's hands pause sifting through the bowl.

"Your father was not bringing you on his papers, mi'ja,
he was bringing you on his wife's.
It was with their combined income, as well as her citizenship,

that your papers would be approved.
She would have to sponsor you
for you to attain a visa & the ability to be a resident.

From what I know, Zoila is not a forgiving woman."
& I think about this wife. I think
I am not a forgiving woman either.

"What's his other daughter's name?" I ask.
Tía fishes through the beans, picking out
the old & wrinkled ones that hold no nutrients.

She is silent in her assessment of the good & bad,
the ones that are allowed to stay, the ones that must be tossed.
I imagine she is plucking through her words with that same
    scrutiny.

"Yahaira. Your sister's name is Yahaira."

———

Twenty-Two Days After

Still reeling   about this sister   about the money.
about my father's secrets, I stop by Carline's house the next day.
The baby is asleep & Carline's eyes are tired,

but when she hugs me, I almost let myself cry
in the warmth of her arms even though
another crying child is the last thing she needs.

We sit on the couch & she does not let go
of my hand. "You already seem like a mother,"
I say, & she laughs, but I'm being honest.

"My breasts ache & I'm always thirsty.
Camino, a group of girls came by to see the baby;
they told me they've seen you at the beach with El Cero.

No me digas que es verdad." I squeeze her hand
before letting it go. "Camino, I would be the last person
to judge you. But El Cero is dangerous."

I nod. Of course he is.
She is not saying anything I don't know.
There is a reason my father paid him to stay away.

There is a reason he keeps circling back to me.
But how can I explain to Carline
something she cannot help me with?

It's just like with Tía; everyone has advice to give,
but all I have to offer her are more worries in response.
The baby's wail stops me from having to say anything.

"Just be careful, Camino.
Now come & greet your nephew."
I ask her if she's given him a name.

"The old women have told me not to,
since his breathing is still so shallow.
But I've decided to call him Luciano."

I hold my best friend's babe, &
I hold her hand as well.
He is premature, but he is loved,

& I know both Carline & I are praying
even though it may seem unlikely,
that that love will be enough.

———

When I next see El Cero in the neighborhood, I treat him like a
     stray;
feed him crumbs of placating attention
that I hope will make him more pet than predator,

but will remind him not to howl at my door.
He always comes back. Pacing near me as I try to ignore him.
Today Vira Lata followed me to the beach.

He sits on my clothes in the warm sun
& keeps a lazy eye on El Cero. He is not
a good guard dog, but I'm still glad not to be alone.

I am packing up my things & El Cero speaks to me.

"Someone asked me for your address recently.
An old friend of your father's. At least he said he was a friend.
But I don't think he was a good man. I told him I didn't know."

I hear the other words El Cero does not say: I can give your
     address
to anyone, I can call attention to you, what protection,
what protection, what protection is a loosely locked gate

& no father   or man   or trained sharp-fanged hound
to stop anyone from breaking   entering.
El Cero cocks his head when I do not respond to him.

He lets a whistle loose through his teeth.
From the clearing, the one that I've walked since I was a child,
an older man comes forth. He has a scar above one eye

& smells like an open sewer that's been sprayed with cologne.
"This is the girl, the one you were asking about.
Camino, this is a friend of your father's."

El Cero hesitates for a second & then grasps my arms.
The man looks me up & down, rubbing his chin.
"I have a few questions, mi amor. Come sit in my car with me."

& all of a sudden I am not sad, or afraid.
I am rage   bow-tied as a girl;
I unfurl, full of fury. I am yelling & I could not tell you what.

I wrench away from El Cero & push the man back hard;
my quick motion excites Vira Lata, who begins barking,
drawing the men's attention as I sprint away.

Angry tears, the first I've shed, stream down my face.
I feel as if I swam too close to a stingray;
my skin vibrates. Electric to the touch.

I turn my back on the beach. I run all the way home.

———

I rush home only to remember tonight is a ceremonial night.

Tía taught me to dance at the ceremonies.
To the drums of the santero. She taught me
a person moves not only with their body but with their spirit.

To the santero's chanting & the chanting of the others.
I watched Tía spin, the colorful beads
around her neck wet with sweat.

Oh! How her waist bent like a willow tree
during the onslaught of a storm.
I learned how low to the ground my knees could get,

how my back could roll & my chest could heave,
my wrapped hair was a plush throne
for the spirits to reign from.

Everyone knew this was a house blessed by saints. & although
a lot of people don't fuck with that kind of thing here,
they were always asking for Tía's remedios & jarabes;

for advice & prayer; for assistance with birthing their babies
when the doctors were too expensive, or when they'd been told,
"There's just nothing else we can do."

& when Tía hosts a ceremony, the crowd outside is legion.
She has a touch, they say, she has the Saints' ears.
Tonight the santero comes, & the practitioners do too.

In our small yard out back the drummers form a circle;
although we are grieving, the songs spring forth full of light.
There is something holy in the night air.

I push the air with my body as if pushing El Cero & his friends.

I pray myself free of pain as I spin in the circle.
I pray myself free of fear as I throw my arms out wide.
I pray myself free with head tosses, with bracelets jangling,

     I pray myself free.

———◆———

CAMINO ✈ YAHAIRA

Everyone in the house
is feeling some type of way.

& since it's only me & Mami,
what I mean is we are tiptoeing around.

Mami pads through the house
writing checks for bills

I didn't even know we had.
Mami is spending money

on a promise; she is spending money
we don't even truly have yet.

She ignores work, forgets appointments.
I do not recognize this reckless woman

who has taken residence in my mother's body.
But I also don't want her to leave

a place I know is safe. So I say nothing.
I make her lunch she doesn't touch,

& I climb through the Johnsons' window
when I need to hear noise around me.

If tension is a winged monster,
it's cast its feathers

on the roof of my house.

———

Twenty-Three Days After

Now that school's done, I walk the streets without purpose.
I walk far north along Riverside Drive.

Sometimes I walk down to Lincoln Center
so I can sit by the fountain.

I avoid dog shit & the people hanging on their stoops;
I ignore ice-cream trucks & hurled catcalls.

I put one foot in front of the other,
& every evening I land at Dre's front door.

Dr. Johnson has wet hands from washing dishes;
she sprays me with water when gesturing me in.

She wraps an arm around my shoulders.
Presses her chin to the top of my head.

I stand there for a second, then step away.
It is nice to be in a home

that feels the same way it did a month ago.
To eat dinner that has no sour reminders.

I let the noises of a whole family lull me into sleep.

Dr. Johnson asks

Yaya, honey, have you been sleeping?

I answer

Kinda, Dr. Johnson

Dr. Johnson asks

Do you want to talk about it?

I answer

Nah, Dr. Johnson

Dr. Johnson asks

Have you talked to anyone about your grief?

I answer

Thanks for the meat loaf, Dr. Johnson

Dr. Johnson asks

Maybe you & your mami?

I answer

Dr. Johnson, I really cannot do this.

Dr. Johnson asks

But couldn't you all give those meetings another try?

I answer

I think I'll go home now.

I never had meat loaf
until the Johnsons moved next door.

It's kinda like a pastelón,
& kinda like a meatball on steroids.

At least once a week
I used to eat at the Johnsons',

even though Mami fussed.
She said the neighborhood would think

she wasn't feeding me.
& I remember thinking Mami was silly

until Doña Gonzales from upstairs
asked me if I was allergic to Mami's cooking.

But besides the busybodies, I've loved
that the Johnsons never minded my presence,

& Dre & I would watch TV after dinner,
or play with her mother's makeup.

But although I love the Johnsons,
I'm not sure I can go back there.

I can't look at Dr. Johnson with her soft, sad eyes.
Despite the relief I felt before in their home

I can't be in a place that's gone on
as if my father never existed.

———

Twenty-Five Days After

My cousin Wilson shows up at the house
on Tuesday afternoon

& sits at the kitchen table,
hugs Mami tight, compliments her hair.

She runs a hand through the strands
that I swear she hasn't washed in four weeks.

Wilson takes a deep breath. Says he wants to marry
his girlfriend, how he's too afraid to ask.

Mami & I look awkwardly at each other,
congratulate him. But Wilson shakes his head.

"A campesino like me, what have I got to offer?"
Wilson has lived in New York City since he was ten.

He's definitely not a campesino anymore.
I don't know any peasant rocking designer sweatpants

& Tom Ford cologne; don't know any rural Dominican
who drinks only expensive whiskey.

But Wilson says the ring he wants to buy his girlfriend
is out of his price range.

& I want to know, what's a bank teller's price range?
& did his girl care about price range when she got with him?

But Mami simply gets up from the table
& grabs her checkbook.

I turn away as she slides the check on the table,
but before I do I see she wrote down four figures.

———

Cucarachas is what I want to call
my mother's family.

How the last few days
they've started creeping up from the woodwork.

These same cousins who called me ugly
want to suck up & say how beautiful I've grown,

how tragic the loss of my father.
The aunts & uncles who said my mom

should have married a lighter-skinned man
all of a sudden want to tell my mother

about this new liposuction procedure they want,
or a church mission trip they've been meaning to take;

a dream wedding they can't afford,
or hospital bills they haven't paid.

Since learning about the advance,
someone new visits every day,

& soon my tongue morphs into a broom:

"Pa' fuera, all of you. Leave us alone.
We are not a fucking bank."

Mami says I'm being rude by turning family away.

   I tell her her family is being rude by asking for money.

Mami says this is what family does, helps each other.

  I tell her our family should be helping us plan the funeral.

Mami doesn't say this is a difficult time.

   I tell her, Mami, I'm not sure you are thinking straight.

Mami looks away from me & gets up to leave the kitchen.

    I ask her what it is she isn't saying.

Mami stops at the doorway, her back to me.

     I brace my arms for impact.

Mami tells me, you always loved him so much.

    I nod silently; at least that much is true.

Mami says, even as smart as you are you ignored the signs.

 I don't ask her what she means, but she keeps talking anyway.

Mami tells me, I wish I'd stopped loving Yano a long time ago.

    I don't have to ask if that's a lie.

Mami tells me, you don't know how he's embarrassed me.

    I want to cover my ears like a little girl—

Mami tells me, & if this death money

   will unshame me with my family, so be it.

CAMINO ✈ YAHAIRA

Twenty-Eight Days After

I have been avoiding the beach for days.
I stretch my arms wide on my bed, & my legs too.
I fan my hair out all around me.

Inside me something has shrunk, but I want to be
deserving of all the space around me. Even as I realize
this space might not be ours for long.

I think about the electric bill for the generator,
the phone bills, the internet bill, the school tuition.
I think about Columbia. I think about New York City.

Tía tells me the funeral will be covered by my father's wife.
My stomach turns over at the thought: my father's secret wife.
My father's secret life. What I've wished & worked for:

sand running through my fingers.

———

I do not ask Tía, but am pretty sure,
this other girl has my same last name.
Papi *was* married to her mother, just like mine.

Yahaira is a great name. & I wonder if he picked it.
I could see my father lovingly saying the syllables.
I search the internet for this name.

It means to light, or to shine. & I wonder
if she was a bulb in my father's heart. I wonder
if she was so bright he kept returning for her

when he could have stayed here with me.
I wonder if she's known about me her whole life.
I wonder if her light was why he was there when she was born.

I'm the child her father left her for in the summers.
While she is the child my father left me for my entire life.
I do not want to hate a girl with a glowing name.

But I cannot help the anger planted in my chest, fanning
its palm leaves wide & casting a shadow on all I've known.
I wonder what kind of girl learns she is almost a millionaire

& doesn't at all wonder about the girl across the ocean
she will be denying food. Tuition. A dream.
Unless she doesn't know about me.

I wonder what college she wants to go to.

I wonder if she will now be able to afford it.

They have ignored me my whole life, those people over there.

But one thing I learned from the Saints,

when the crossroads are open to you, you must decide a path.

I will not stand still while the world makes my choices.

This Yahaira

will learn

what carving your own way means.

———

Social media seemed like the easiest way to search
two hours ago, but with so many girls named Yahaira Rios
I haven't stopped scrolling faces

trying to find a girl who looks like me.
I am about to quit when I see a profile
but the picture is only a black box, & the date

                                      my father died.
Although the profile is private,
I can see some posts, including condolence messages.

"Tío Yano was a great man. He's in heaven now, RIP,"
a boy named Wilson has written. "I will always miss Pops,"
writes a girl named Andrea. & my heart thumps in my chest,

& my fingers shake over the tablet as I press the message button.
I write a quick sentence & press Send before I can stop myself.
There is no way she can't know who I am once she sees it.

———

After I send the message,
I refresh the page
at least fifty times waiting for a response.

I walk into the kitchen to get some crackers.
I wash some dishes that are in the sink.
I dust the altar. Refill the vases with fresh water.

Then return to my tablet.

Still no response.
There is no time difference where my sister is,
which means it is late afternoon.

Maybe she is busy
being rich & hanging out with her mother
& not thinking about me.

I check the message one more time.
It does not show it's been read.
It does not show it's been opened.

I almost wish I could unsend the message.
But no, she deserves to read it.
I deserve to know & be known.

I turn off my tablet.

———

Tía & I go to El Malecón, where my parents re-met.
She carries a fresh jar of molasses & a watermelon;
I haul the honeyed rum. La Virgen de Regla loves sweets.

Tía & I pray over the offerings; reciting the names
of our ancestors. We kiss the rind, the jar, the glass bottle
holding the rum.

We touch these items to our foreheads,
then we touch them to our hearts. I breathe the salty air,
the rush of waves against stone joins us in our prayers.

We pour a bit of homemade mamajuana into the water,
& Tía doesn't even stop me when I take a sip from the bottle.
I am feeling guilty. I wonder if the girl in New York

didn't know about me, if a random message online
might be a heavy thing to carry.
At least I had Tía's honest & open face tell me the truth,

not a random pixelated image. I pour my thick guilt
into the water as well. The patron saint of the ocean
is known for containing many parts of herself:

she is a nurturer, but she is also a ferocious defender.
& so I remember that to walk this world
you must be kind but also fierce.

———

After our trip to El Malecón,
I walk back home & straight into my room.
I pull out my tablet & turn it back on.

My breath catches in my chest.
I search social media—
still no notification.

I stop myself just before
I throw the tablet at the wall.
I was not born to patience.

———

I grab a sack
& load it with
a small bag of rice

& one of beans.
Soon, I don't know how
Tía & I will eat,

but for now
we still have more
than the other people

who live here.
I walk to Carline's.
Waving to neighbors,

avoiding potholes,
letting the sun
warm the skin on my back.

At her house,
Maman ushers me in,
her eyes tired,

& when I look at Carline
I can tell she's been crying.
I pass the sack to Maman,

giving her an extra-tight hug
hoping it offers comfort.
She hugs me tightly back,

& for a second
I think she is also
offering comfort to me.

When she walks out back
to el fogón,
the open fire where she cooks,

I sit on the couch
& gently pull Luciano
from Carline & onto my chest.

I can tell she
doesn't want to let him go,
but also that she needs a moment

to collect herself.
I do not ask what happened.
She tells me herself.

"I lost my job.
They wanted me to start coming in.
But how could I leave him so soon? How?"

I nod along,
humming to Luciano.
His lashes flutter

against his small dark cheek.
I read somewhere
that even this little,

when they sleep babies can dream.

Since I do not have my father's pull,
I cannot make empty promises
about jobs or positions I can get for Carline.

"I just wish I could stay with my baby.
If only I could make miracles like Tía."
Tía already has an apprentice. Me.

& even I cannot wield miracles the way she can.

I don't want to make light
of what Carline just told me.
I also know she needs a distraction.

So I tell her about my sister.
I tell her I reached out.
Carline gasps at all the right moments

& clutches my hand.
She nods in agreement.
"You did what you had to do, Camino."

I am not the kind of girl
who looks for approval.
But a weight lifts off my chest.

I did what must be done.

———◆———

The last time I saw my parents kiss
I was pretty small.

        But it's still hard to hear
that your own mother wasn't happy.

Papi was always smiling, always full
of words & joy.

        I wish I knew the rift
that grew this sea between them.

I used to think it was me, that Papi
& I had chess.

That maybe Mami was jealous
it wasn't something she shared.

But even when I started painting nails
& asking about her job

Mami still had an air around Papi,
like he was a medicine she knew she needed

even as she cringed at the taste.

But now I wonder
if it was always more than that.

Maybe Mami knew about the other woman?
Even without seeing the certificate.

I think of how the word *unhappy* houses
so many unanswered questions.

———

Thirty-One Days After

Tía Lidia comes to dinner Monday night.
It is mostly silent until she asks me about my college essay;

I mention I'm rethinking the schools I want to apply to.
Mami looks up from her plate of arroz con guandules,
    surprised.

"Just because I'm not your father doesn't mean I don't care.
You didn't tell me you scrapped your list, Yahaira.

We only have each other, you know. & he,
he always had more people in his life than he needed."

Her tone is a serrated knife.
                    I become a feast of anger.

But before I can reply to her
she throws her fork down on the plate & leaves,

dragging her footsteps so her chancletas slur drunkenly to her
    room.
Tía Lidia puts her hand over mine. "Your mother is having

a tough time. Their marriage wasn't easy, & she has so much
she's dealing with. Yano was a great father to *you*,

& I know you loved him, but he wasn't always a great husband."
& I don't know how one man can be so many different things

to the people he was closest to. But I nod. I almost slip & ask
does everyone know? But if they don't I can't be the one

to reveal the dirt on my father's name.

—●—

Once, I had a tournament in Memphis.
Both Mami & Papi came.

It's a happy memory. Not just because I won
but because we went on a boat tour

of the Mississippi River. & the sun shone bright,
& the tour guide had this amazing voice

that made you want to lean into his words.
& he kept saying, "Ships have gone down in this water,

gold has been lost here, the banks have eroded,
cities have been built & destroyed at its shores,

tribes have crossed it & never crossed back.
But the Mississippi rises & falls; it rises & falls.

Everything changes, but the water rises & falls."
& for some reason, I think of that memory

& that tournament as Mami huffs around the house.
Some things continue forever. Maybe anger is like a river,

maybe it crumbles everything around it, maybe it hides
so many skeletons beneath the rolling surface.

Thirty-Five Days After

For the first time in weeks, I log on to social media.
I have comments from friends.

I have reminders of birthdays & events,
& I have one new friend request

from a girl I don't know in Sosúa, Dominican Republic.
She has my same last name: Rios. Camino Rios.

She is slightly lighter complexioned
than my velvet brown,

her eyes are big & piercing,
& her smile looks familiar.

There is a message with the request,
but I can't stop looking at her profile picture.

Because this Camino girl isn't alone in the photo;
she is in a red bathing suit, my father's arm

thrown around her shoulders
as they laugh in the sunlight.

An awful sinking feeling
almost stops my breath.

———————

A feeling I cannot name is growing in my chest.
It is large & large & large

& before it expands inside my throat
& chokes me, I yell for Mami.

She shuffles into the room
with more speed than I've seen her

      demonstrate in days.
      I point to the screen:

"Have you ever seen this picture?
 I don't know this girl. Why is he with this girl?"

On a hard breath, she slaps her hand
against her chest, as if trying to press

a pause button on her heart.

"Who is this, Ma? A cousin
I don't know about? Who is this?"

But I can see my guesses are wrong.
"I know he was your hero, Yahaira.

& I tried my best
to make sure he would remain so.

But that girl   that girl is the daughter
from your father's other family."

———◆———

My father not only had another wife.
He also had another child.

I have to close my laptop because
all my shaking hands want to do

is sweep the entire thing off my desk.
I want to see the image of my father

& this girl shattered against the floor.
How could an entire person exist

who shares half my DNA
& no one thought to tell me?

In all the time I held
what I thought was a massive secret

I never imagined there could be a child
from my father's secret marriage.

Or perhaps, my father's not-so-secret marriage
since it seems everyone else still knew

more than me   even Mami
who I was trying to protect.

It's taken me almost twelve months
to deal with the truth of who my father was

but even that was a lie. My stomach churns,
& I feel myself about to be sick.

I bend my face forward, & Mami puts
a hand on my back. But I pull away from her.

All these lies that we've all swallowed,
they're probably rotting in our stomachs.

———

"I knew about his wife," I tell Mami.
"I can't believe no one told me."

She shakes her head. "But how?
We didn't want to burden you."

I wave my hand at the computer.
"This I didn't know about.

This—*person*—I couldn't imagine."
I am taking big, gasping breaths.

Mami does not try to rub my back again,
but she gently whispers to me:

"Respira, Yahaira, respira.
Así, nice, big breaths."

I feel like a spool of thread
that's been dropped to the ground.

I'm rolling undone
from the truth of this thing.

A sister. A sister. A sister.

———

Ma tries to explain things to me,
but I feel like I've been dropped

into a part of the story
where all of the characters are unfamiliar.

"She was my friend. His other wife.
I actually met him through her."

He married the other woman
after her, so it wasn't technically legal.

But the other woman didn't know that
until much, much later.

Mami married my father
against her own father's wishes.

My maternal grandfather was high up in the military
& wanted Mami to marry someone of rank.

My mother says she almost died
when she learned of Papi's betrayal.

All the people she dismissed when marrying Papi,
only to have him betray her a few months after they wed.

She cannot get through the story
without her voice breaking

my entire heart. & then she tells me
what I did not expect.

"She's dead, his wife. Did you know?
Almost ten years ago. Your father never got over it.

Neither did I. I used to wish she'd go away,
but it was unthinkable, the way it happened."

I want to hate this dead woman. For the way
even talking about her twists up my mother's face.

This dead woman, who made my father visit,
& have a child, & board a plane   that fell into the ocean.

I am slow to put the pieces together.
I want to hate a dead woman, & her daughter

who most likely hates me for making my father
leave her in the first place.

———◆———

Without thinking, I ask Mami why.

Mami sifts through her thoughts
as if trying to figure out what I'm really asking.

& I mean all of it. Why would Papi
do this to her? To us?

> "He told me once, with me,
> he felt like he had to perform,

> become a character in a play,
> he had to prove he was good enough.

> That he had earned the right
> to marry the heralded general's only child.

> But with her, with the woman who was my friend,
> who was *his* childhood friend, he could take off

> the mask.

> I was an aspiration, a flame he wanted to kiss.
> But for her, he would have lit the entire island.

> I was a smart decision. She made a dreamer of him.
> & well, for the child that came, he sacrificed it all.

He loved you both. Understand that.
A part of me even thinks he might have loved me

& his other wife too.
Yano was a complicated man.

After she died, I refused to have the child here.
It was all too much. I don't know! I can't explain.

Your father refused not to be in her life;
he would not abandon her completely.

I know now,
I should not ever have asked it of him.

So he created a theater of his life
& got lost in all the different roles he had to play."

———————

Mami seems so tired
after telling me what she knows

& I feel so tired just
hearing it. I do not

want to speak to Mami
anymore. She must

realize I need a break
from her, from this, because

she kisses me good night
& only sighs when I

do not say the words back.
I know, in the place

inside me that is still clear
& fair, this is not my mother's

fault. But I'm just so damn
tired of being lied to, & she

is the only one who is here
for me to be angry at.

I sit & stare at the message
Camino Rios sent me.

I sit & stare at the picture
of my father proudly hugging

a child that is not me.
I could delete the message.

I *should* delete the message.
Why say a single thing

to this girl I do not know?
I will decline her friend request.

———

CAMINO ✈ YAHAIRA

When I get home from picking up my report card
there is a notification shining blue
on my tablet.

It's been days since I sent the message.

I stopped believing she'd ever see it.
I stopped checking it incessantly.
But now, here is a response.

Tía asks me if I want something to eat

but I feel so queasy, I don't think I could.
I unlock the tablet & take a deep breath.
There is shock in the list of questions

the girl, Yahaira, has sent my way.
& it is clear she did not know
I existed.

———

Message from Yahaira Rios:

How old are you?
Did Papi live with you when he visited?

Where in the Dominican Republic do you live?
Have you ever been to the States?

Who do you live with there?
Do you have other siblings?

How did you learn Papi had died?
I think we need to video-chat.

———

As far back as I've had memory to keep me company,
It's been Tía & me making an existence.
Papi, someone who was only present by voice & pixelated face,

& by his summer visits that were always too short.
I was not the kind of child who wanted siblings,
or someone to play with my hair.

Sometimes, I would miss the mother I barely knew,
but mostly, Tía was all the parent I needed;
all the family I thought I wanted.

It is strange to go from being an only child
to seeing someone wearing your own face.
Now there is this other person & supposedly she is my sister

where yesterday she was just a name
holding the future I thought I wanted;
now there is a girl of blood & flesh who is

second only to Tía as the closest thing I have to family.

———●———

I do not reply to her.
Even though I know
the message will show as read.

I take a moment to figure out
what it is I want to say.
I am nervous to admit to Tía what I've done.

That I've reached out
& told her my father's secret:

I   Exist.

I must make a sound.
Because Tía looks up from her reading
or maybe in her magic way, she just knows.

Our backyard rooster crows an evening song.

"I reached out to Yahaira. Papi's girl. She responded."
Tía puts down her book but is otherwise silent.
"She wants to talk. She wants to video-chat."

& it comes as a surprise to me,
but all of a sudden I'm crying, the sob
pulled up from the well in my chest,

full & wet, & Tía must have been expecting it.
She scoops me to her.
"Ya, mi'ja, ya. Ya, mi'ja, ya."

What I respond
to this Yahaira:
Hello. Yes.

We should talk.

———

"You're in this square
& squares don't overlap."

Papi taught me every piece
has its own space.

Papi taught me every piece
moves in its own way.

Papi taught me every piece
has its own purpose.

The squares do not overlap.
& neither do the pieces.

The only time two pieces
stand in the same square

is the second before one
is being taken & replaced.

& I know now, Papi could not
move between two families.

When he was here—he was mine,
when he was there he was theirs.

He would glide from family to family,
square to square & never look back.

It's why I heard so little from him
when he was gone.

It's why the girl in DR
needed to message me

to confirm I am my father's daughter.
Everything has a purpose, Papi taught me.

But what was his   in keeping
such   big   secrets?

———————

Thirty-Six Days After

We eat in silence. We haven't sat
at the dinner table since Papi.

Instead, we bring plates to the couch
& pretend to eat with them in our laps.

I haven't seen Mami wear makeup
in weeks, & her chancletas

are the only footwear she rocks these days.
Between commercials I play on my phone.

Now that school's out, I don't even have
homework to distract me from the silence

which is why I'm surprised today
when Mami mutes her novela to say

"We need to make plans for your future;
we are the only family we have left."

Because Mami did not want to legally fight Papi's will,
after Papi's remains are released to us

he'll be flown back to DR to be buried.
Mami refuses to talk about the body.

After she goes to bed, I begin doing research
on what I would need to travel.

It is funny how money has no regard for time.
How it eases past minutes to get you what you want.

Thankfully, I have a passport. Papi had me get one years ago
when it became clear I might qualify for tournaments abroad.

For a ticket, I used Mami's credit card.
Mami does not remove any passwords from our computer,

& I log on to her bank account & ensure we have enough.

I still don't know if I have the courage
to do what I want to do, & I know I can't plan this trip alone

but somehow, some way, I know I need to be there
the day that Papi gets buried. I need to meet this sister.

———————

I don't know
how much of

my desire
to meet Camino

is because
all of a sudden

I have a sister,
& that's very

What the fuck?
But also, maybe,

a part of me feels
that she is a piece

of Papi.
That in her body

there will be answers
for all the questions

he left behind.
How could she

have existed
this whole time

without me?
Me without her?

Nothing has been logical
since the morning

Mami came to school,
but in my heart

of hearts I know
whatever I need to find

I'll need to go.

———•———

Thirty-Seven Days After

Mami has not asked me again
about the online message.

& I have not given
her any updates.

I told Dre because holding it in
was killing me.

She shook her head & pushed
a loud whistle through her teeth.

"Damn, who would have thought
Poppa Rios had it in him?"

After a moment she said,
"Maybe it's better you didn't know?"

How can you lose
an entire person,

only to gain a part of them back
in someone entirely new?

"I think I need to go meet her,
with Papi's body, I mean."

Dre nods without hesitation.
"Yes. It's the right thing to do."

& although her words
should be a comfort,

a twinge of annoyance twists
my mouth. How could she

possibly know the right thing
to do? In a situation like this,

how would anyone know
so easily right from wrong

when it all seems like we are
pivoting left, spinning in circles.

CAMINO ✈ YAHAIRA

I think I hate this sister.
She messages me
that she has acquired a plane ticket.

& how easy she says it.
Because it wasn't endless paperwork,
because no one wondered if she would

want to overstay her visa.
The years my father tried
to get me to the States,

& that girl over there fills out a short form,
is granted permission, given a blue book—
shit, an entire welcome mat to the world.

I squeeze my tablet so hard
I'm surprised I don't crack the screen.
Her mother will not let her come, & she is planning

to do so behind her back.
That takes strength. I know if it were me,
Tía would kill me dead,

then have the spirits bring me back to life
so she could murder me all over again.
As much as I want to hate this girl,

I also have to admire what she will do to get here.
& I hope that she will admire
all I will do to get there, too.

———

Forty Days After

It's been three weeks since Carline gave birth.
I visit her every few days. Today carrying
vitamins & cloth diapers on top of my head,

                I let my arms swing freely.
When I was little, my mother told me
she used to carry bundles of mangoes

to the market this way.
On mornings like this I pretend I'm her:
a girl who can carry water on her crown,

who can walk barefoot without being scorched.
Although, I'm wearing a pair of Jordans that I now think
were probably my sister's first;

they were not new when Papi
brought them to me, & I think back to all the hand-me-downs
I didn't know were that other girl's castoffs.

When I get to the house, Carline is there alone.
She chews on a thumbnail while little Luciano
sleeps quietly in a crib. In another country,

this baby would still be in the intensive care unit,
but these are Kreyòl-speaking folk who cannot afford
either the bill or the legalities that would come with hospitals.

Although Carline will not utter the words,
I know she still expects the baby to die.
He is just so, so small.

———

Carline takes the bundle from me slowly
& unwraps it like it might contain precious gems.
I ask her if I can wake the baby to check if he's doing all right.

Tía has taught me how to listen to the babies' hearts & swab
their throats for mucus. She has taught me how to feel
the neck for fever, to look for infection where the cord was cut.

Carline nods but gives me a long look. & I know her eyes
are telling me to be careful. We are friends, but she
is a mother now, & she is wary of anyone hurting her child.

She tells me Nelson is working himself to the bone
trying to save enough to move them out
& is also considering dropping out of school.

I want to offer her platitudes & murmurs
that it will all be all right. But thing is,
this isn't an uncommon story.

A lot of people don't finish school
or follow their dreams. That fairy-tale plotline is for
telenovelas.

Instead of saying soft, nice words, I fold clean towels
& stack dirty dishes. I sweep & make myself useful.
It is the best kind of gift I can offer Carline.

———

My father having two families
is also not an uncommon story.
When Yahaira messaged me

she seemed unutterably betrayed.

As if she couldn't believe this of Papi.
But me, I know a man can have many faces & speak out of
both sides of his mouth; I know a man can make decisions

based on the flip of a coin;
a man can be real good at long division,
give away piece after piece after piece of himself.

I do not tell Carline any of this. I hand her back the child.
I promise to check on her again next week.
She asks me if I heard back about the message I sent,

but I do not know how to pucker my mouth
around the words I want to say. What does another burden
do for Carline? & a part of me feels shame.

It is then I know, my father has become a secret,
even from my dearest friend. He's become
an unspeakable name.

All I want
is Papi back.
I want his

booming laugh
to shake the walls.
I want his heavy

knock to the
outside door.
I want his

stupid sayings,
& his angry bellow,
& his mixed-up English

he would pepper
in conversation
& his eyes

that misted over
when he prayed
or when he danced.

There are pieces
of him all over
this barrio,

all over
República Dominicana,
& beyond that

to New York City,
but I can't bundle
those pieces.

Can't tie them tight with twine;
can't blow life into them,
or shed light onto them

or assemble those pieces
to make anything, anyone,
resembling him.

———

The news no longer shares
updates about the plane crash;
there are more important

or current tragedies to cover.
Throughout the neighborhood,
people keep candles lit in windows,

& every time I walk by a storefront
someone tips their hat
& asks if I need anything.

The rest of the world has moved on
to bigger & juicier news;
so many of us here seem suspended

in time, still waiting for more
information, still hoping
this is a nightmare we'll wake from.

———

Forty-Two Days After

My skin itches from missing the sea.
I force myself to help Tía with her cough syrups
& making her rounds until

I snicker one time too many beneath my breath.

Tía waves her hand in my face. "Te fuiste lejo."
& she's right. My mind drifted off far away.
"When was the last time you went swimming?

You're just like your mother.
She was always happiest when she was near the water.
It's why she loved visiting El Malecón."

& I know I can't avoid the water forever, especially not now.
In my room I hold my swimsuit up to my nose
& the scent of laundry soap is a small comfort.

———

What are arms in the water if not wings?
I slice through the liquid sky.
Push the water behind me.

I move with a speed
I've never moved with before.
Out into the ocean & back.

Until my wings again become arms
that are aching
& my lungs need big gulps of air.

I push onto my back & float.
The curved spoon of moon
peeks through clouds.

When I open my eyes
to the sand, there he is.
There he always fucking is.

"You were swimming
as if demons were chasing
with torches behind you."

I roll my shoulders
before walking calmly to
shimmy into my shorts.

Pretend not to see
El Cero checking out my ass
from where he's crouching.

———

"Is this where
you want me, Camino?
Begging at your feet?"

The body is a funny piece of meat.
How it inflates & deflates
in order to keep you alive,

but how simple words can fill you up
or pierce the air out of you.
El Cero gives me more goose bumps

than freezing water. & never the
kind that means you're moved.
Always the kind that means

run hard & fast in the other direction.

"I don't want anything from you."
But he shakes his head almost sadly.
"You need me."

Leave me alone, Cero. Just leave me the hell alone.

On my way home from the beach I get caught in the rain.
Tía is stirring an asopao in a huge pot; the rice & meat stew
fills the house

with the scent
of bay leaves. She gives me a look & points her large metal spoon
at my tablet. "That thing has been chirping, & you're lucky

I didn't put it on the porch so this rain could shut it up.
Turn the volume down on that thing." Although Papi
was not her brother,

she'd known him forever. I have yet to ask her
how she's doing. The notifications on my tablet
pop up in long succession.

Esa Yahaira wants to video-chat. & the thought of that
makes my palms sweaty.
What will I see in the face of this girl? Am I ready to see it?

———————

Yahaira & I are supposed
to video-chat after dinner.
But the appointed time has passed,

& I still dawdle in the kitchen,
washing dishes & putting away the leftovers
in recycled margarine containers.

Tía shuffles to her room to watch a novela
& shuts her door. I take my tablet to the porch
although the tiles are still wet,

although the Wi-Fi is faintest here.
It's almost as if I want a reason
not to speak to the girl.

I have missed two calls.
& five minutes later my tablet chimes.
The porch light is faint, but when I answer,

the light behind the girl
is bright bright bright.
& as her face comes into focus my heart stops.

She has Papi's face.
His tight curls. His broad nose.
Her lips are shaped different but full like his.

My sister is pretty. Darker than me,
& clearly eating better, yet
I know that strangers in the street

would look at us
& peg easily that we are related;
we are of the same features.

Neither of us says a word.
On the screen, beyond where she can see my hand,
I trace her chin with my finger.

& for the first time
I don't just feel loss.
I don't feel just a big gaping

hole at everything
my father's absence has consumed.
Look at what it's spit out & offered.

Look at who it's given me.

CAMINO ✈ YAHAIRA

Camino is like a golden version of me,
with long loose curls hanging wet down her back.

She tells me she likes to swim & was at the beach.
She has the look of a swimmer, long limbed, thin.

She doesn't smile much on the call,
& I press my shaky hands together;

I don't want her to see that I'm nervous.
We don't spend much time chitchatting.

In fact, for the first couple of seconds,
we are completely silent.

I memorize her features
& puzzle-piece her face, see my own there

& Papi's. I compare what our mothers must have given us.
But I suspect if I say any of this out loud Camino will shut down.

She does not offer me many long sentences;
& her face shows no enthusiasm to connect.

She seems like she is not the type to deal with emotions well.
So I move to what I know how to do: strategy.

I outline what I'm thinking, my plans for attending
the funeral. & then I tell her what I'll need from her.

She is silent a moment. Slow to agree.
& the way her forehead wrinkles

looks just like Papi's used to when he was trying to figure out
if I had laid a trap down for his king to fall into.

Finally she nods.

———

Forty-Three Days After

I can't remember the last time
Mami & I went shopping together.

We don't got the same taste at all;
every Christmas & birthday Mami will buy me

cute little rompers & low-cut shirts & I'll have to throw
on leggings under   or a button-down on top.

Not that I don't look cute,
but just that our styles don't necessarily match.

& it's easy to remember why. Mami
is a showpiece of a woman. Her long hair

sleek & shiny down to the middle of her back,
jeans tighter than mine, tight shirt too.

She doesn't look like an American-apple-pie mother.
She looks like a tres golpes of a mother.

& I've forgotten that these last weeks she's piled her hair into
     rollers
& rocked nothing but dusty sweats & slippers.

But it is obvious now, as dudes eye her as we walk
(*I* walk, Mami swishes her big butt).

She's just every kind of feminine,
& I've never been sure I'd measure up.

Camino would probably be thought her daughter before me.
I grab Mami's hand & move closer to her.

A childish move, I know. But a reminder to all of us,
she is mine. & only mine.

———•———

"You ever wish I looked more like you?
That people looked at you &

didn't have to wonder at our relationship?"
Mami looks startled by the question.

"Y esa ridícule? What you mean, looked more like me?
You look just like me. Your heart-shaped mouth,

your fat big toe, your ears like seashells;
your eyes same brown as mine.

You got your father's coloring, kinked hair,
& stubbornness, but the rest of you is all me.

& anyone that can't see that que se vayan al carajo."

Mami is annoyed. I can tell by the pinched jawline.
The same way my jaw looks pinched when I'm annoyed.

"Everyone always said I looked just like Papi."

For some reason I want to keep pushing her.
I want her to defend all the parts of her that live in me.

"Ay, Mamita." Mami's face smooths out.
We are standing still on the sidewalk,

& the hustle & bustle of Grand Concourse,
the people running in & out of shops, fade away;

the heat sticks to our bodies, a second skin.
I take a deep, warm breath.

———

"People loved to say you were your father's daughter.

& you, you loved to hear it. I'm sure you've always thought
me silly or superficial, or qué sé yo, too girly?

You, you've always been the best of daughters.
& already so beautiful. So good at makeup & funky clothes.

O, ¡pero claro! I wish you would straighten your hair more.
But I also understand your style doesn't have to be my own.

I have my fingerprints all over you.
& I don't need the world to see them

to know that they're there."

———

Although Mami is dead-ass serious
that she isn't going to the DR funeral,

she is the one who visits the morgue
when we are given custody of what is left of Papi's body;

she is the one who decides what to do with the remains.

Who takes Papi's favorite navy blue suit to the mortician.
She is the one who comes home ashy gray in the face.

Who does not describe
what the leftovers look like, only hugs me to her.

She is the one who says, "Thank goodness
for that damn gold tooth."

She is the one who calls the Dominican Republic
& says, "It needs to be a closed casket;

whatever you do, don't let the girl see what is left."
& I know she means Camino, means to spare her.

I don't understand my parents' kind of love & hate.
What it must take for Mami to lose him all over.

But I know she must have love for him, right?
She is so, so tender when she irons & folds

the purple pocket square that will go inside his grave.

———

Papi will have two funerals.
Papi will have two ceremonies.

Papi will be mourned in two countries.
Papi will be said goodbye to here & there.

Papi had two lives.
Papi has two daughters.

Papi was a man split in two,
playing a game against himself.

But the problem with that
is that in order to win, you also always lose.

———•———

All I want
is my father back.

I want his heavy

footsteps to tread
outside my door.

I want his
stupid sayings,

& his angry bellow,
& rapid Spanish,

& his eyes
that misted over

when his favorite
song played.

There are pieces
of him all over

the house,
all over New York City,

& beyond that to the island,
but I can't bundle

them together
to make anything,

anyone
resembling him.

———

CAMINO ✈ YAHAIRA

Forty-Five Days After

The school year ended weeks ago. I've hidden three bills
the school's sent beneath a candle Tía never moves.
I'm hoping the Saints will step in.

I don't know how I'll pay for it. But my sister & her mother
are rich, & damn if they don't owe me something.
I just hope Tía doesn't find the bills first.

In a week & some change, July 29, I will turn seventeen.
The same day my father's remains will be buried.
I don't know if my sister knows

that day is my birthday. & I don't tell her.
At the beach I swim until I hit the resort buoys, then swim back.
& mostly ignore El Cero watching from the water bank.

He's started taking out his phone
& recording me on the beach
I do not want to think what he does with these videos.

I help Tía with her rounds of the neighborhood.
We visit the lady with cancer & wipe her brow.
I sit with Carline & her baby.

I count down the days to the end of July.

———————

Forty-Six Days After

Four days before my sister is supposed to arrive,
I finally get my nerve up. I call her after dinner.
She answers with a smile. I know it will not last.

"I won't tell you any details about the funeral
unless you transfer me money. You'll show up
for nothing. My Tía won't help you sneak over here."

I don't want to be brisk. It almost hurts me to look
into her wide, soft eyes & ask for so so much.
But her softness has nothing to do with the desperation

I feel growing inside me. After Papi's burial
I will have to leave this place. There is nothing
for me in this town where I see my exit doors growing smaller.

My words, weighed down, become an avalanche.
In the blink of a second Yahaira's face goes blank.
She leans back in her seat. "Of course. It's your money too.

You didn't have to threaten me to ask for it.
We haven't gotten the advance in full,
but how much would you like me to transfer?"

I don't know if it's her cool tone or my guilt that causes me to
     flinch.

She can say whatever she wants, but no one,
no one gives you something simply for asking.
Life is an exchange; you'd think a chess player would know that.

"Ten thousand. You can keep everything else."

I swallow back the bile that rises in my mouth.
I will make it alone on my own two feet. I give Yahaira
the information to wire cash. She promises to do it this week.

I hang up the phone without saying goodbye.
It seems easiest not to get attached to this sister,
to not give her a single reason to get attached to me.

———

Yahaira sends me the money & her flight plans.
She bought the flight with a credit card
that her mother doesn't check.

She asks if I can pick her up from the airport.
& I want to ask her what car she thinks I have.
Or maybe she imagines like a mule

I will sling her across my back?
I may be a pobrecita right now,
but I am no one's errand girl.

Perhaps she thinks she's bought my compliance?
Perhaps that's what I implied.
But I am annoyed to be treated like a servant girl.

All that money & she can't just order a taxi?

But honestly, the taxi drivers are thieves.
& what if something happened to her,
a gringuita alone? Tía would kill me.

My father's ghost would probably haunt me.
My guilt for sure would. I already feel horrible
about the money that was transferred to Western Union.

I picked up the fat envelope yesterday & taped it
to Papi's picture on Tía's altar in the living room.
So I tell her I will be at the airport.

I don't tell her I'm unsure how I'll be getting there.

Is this what sisterhood is?
A negotiation of the things you make possible
out of impossible requests?

———

CAMINO ✈ YAHAIRA

Mami won't let me see the real remains.

The airline representative mails us
a catalog of all the bits of cloth,

& bone & hair & suitcase things
that probably belong to my father.

I stare at the photos. All the bits & pieces
that will be buried of Papi.

& I think about everything my father
left behind that won't be in that box:

the swollen questions
that are bursting the seams of our lives.

The huge absence that stretches over
every waking moment.

The disrepaired—the broken that fell apart
long before his plane did.

I look at the scraps of a body
they have piled into a casket & called a man.

I know the remains are strewn around us.
In this everyday life of the left over.

———

Forty-Nine Days After

Before Papi is shipped to DR
Mami decides we need to hold a wake.

The funeral parlor that will ship his body
prepares for the event. No viewing.

Although Tío Jorge
seems upset with Mami

for how she spoke to him last time,
he picks us up for the wake.

When he opens the car door for me,
he grabs me up in a tight, tight hug.

I find it hard to look at him,
to smell his scent. Sometimes

if I let myself forget my father is dead
I can look at Tío Jorge & see him here

standing before me, looking so much like my father.

Tears are gathered in his eyes.
& in his choked voice.

He waves a hand in front of his face
as if it will clear both.

He tells me "I love you, Yaya. Bella negra."
I bury my face in his neck & to myself I whisper,

Bella negra. Bella negra.
Papi's right here. He's with us.

Papi was embalmed in sea salt,
like an ancient insect caught in honey,

unmoving, from a different time.
Papi was always in motion,

his smile bursting forth,
bursting the way my heart feels

when I kneel at his casket
& every big emotion inside me

makes my chest shake.
But I blink away tears,

& I throw my shoulders back.

"Never let them see you sweat.
& even if you have to forfeit, smile."

———•———

As Mami & I sit in the front row,
people come up to us to pay their respects.

Such a funny phrase, *pay respects*.
As if suffering is a debt that can be eased

by a hug & a head nod.
I have no need for this currency of people's respect:

My cousins shuffle awkwardly
from foot to foot.

Dre, with Dr. Johnson beside her, sits behind me,
her hands in her lap ready to jump to my rescue.

Wilson stands with his fiancée in the back of the funeral parlor,
his big hands full of white carnations.

I cannot fold any of their respects into my dress's pockets.

I cannot tie these respects together into a bouquet
to lay at my father's headstone.

Their respects are quick-footed
& I am sludging through this hardened mud of loss.

———

Wilson is wearing a black button-down
& slacks, & on a different day,

I would joke that he looks like he's
going to a job interview.

But, today, my father is dead.
His body that held so much noise is in a box.

& so I don't diss Wilson,
I don't reach for his hand;

I give him a small smile
& sit with my mother.

Papi always liked Wilson, & I wonder:
would he have been upset Wilson asked for money?

I'm not sure he would have been. He was a generous man.

I wonder if maybe I should be less angry
about something neither one of my parents

would have been angry about. But I don't know.
I could always anticipate Papi's moves.

His every feeling flashed across his face
like the digital ads at the bus stops.

For the rest of my life I will sit & imagine
what my father would say in any given moment.

& I will make him up:
his words, his advice, our memories.

Tomorrow morning the funeral director

will ship the body out to DR; ship the body,
as if it is an Amazon order of toilet paper or textbooks.

People come & people leave.
But Dre stays until the very end,

presses drooping carnations
into my hands, & I know she bought them

outside the train station & carried them
through rush hour & bus transfers & a walk

to give them to me. "I just wanted you
to have something . . ."

& the knot in my throat swells to twice its size,
my tongue bloated & still in the coffin of my mouth.

I nod & take them from her.
She gives my shoulder a small squeeze.

They are beautiful. I love them. I love you.
You are the only thing that does not hurt.

I try to say with my eyes since I can't
get my mouth to make a single sound.

———————

I don't want to tell Dre
I am accompanying my father's body,

but since I can't keep a single secret from her
I blurt it out anyway. & then ask her not to ask me anything.

"I knew you were going
but lying to your moms is too much."

Dre shakes her head with frustration.
"I hope you know what you're doing, Yaya.

We aren't like white girls in movies
who fly off & have adventures. This sounds reckless."

I want to agree with her, I do;
I even nod. But all I can think

is that it seems wild to me
that our family would let Papi fly alone again.

As if dying alone wasn't enough.
Nah. I don't tell Dre a thing.

Not as she helps me clean & collect
the condolence cards,

as Mami makes arrangements for the flowers
that will never rest at a grave.

At one point, Dre holds my hand
gently in hers, & it thaws

a part of me I didn't even know
had been left cold.

A funeral parlor is not a romantic place
or a warm place or a place to cuddle.

Especially when it's your own father's death
you are there to mourn.

But curl into Dre is exactly what I want to do.

"Can I sleep over later?"
I ask her, my hand still in hers.

She gives it a squeeze. "I'd love that,
but maybe you should talk to your mom?

She seems really upset,
& you know how she is about that kind of thing."

Mami hates the concept of sleepovers,
says our house has enough beds

& what kind of sheets does someone else have
that I cannot sleep in my own?

———————

I know what ugly looks like
when it departs from your mouth fully formed.

How the words can push space between two people;
how it's close to impossible to collapse that space.

After the viewing, we are in a cab headed back to Morningside,
& I am hoping Mami does not say anything

but of course   she does   utter words:
"I think we should take a trip. For your birthday.

I think we need to get away. Somewhere far, far.
He would have wanted you to celebrate."

& I don't say my father also would have wanted
me at his funeral. She knows this.

I understand she's angry at him. I am too.
But my father was a man of commemorations;

no way he would have wanted to be buried
without his child there to make sure they lowered

his casket properly; that they laid the bouquet of flowers
over his grave with the appropriate amount of respect.

& now I know my feelings flash across my face.
That is the dumbest transition I've ever heard.

Who is thinking about a birthday when they're thinking
about a funeral? What could I want? What could I want?

"That's stupid to think about.
I just want to be left alone."

& there goes that ugly again. Like a picket fence risen
between us; we can still see each other,

but it's a barrier too high to climb.

———————

I tell Mami
I'm sleeping over

at Dre's house.

I do not ask
for permission,

& although her jaw
tightens,

she does not say
a word to me.

I climb through
Dre's window,

hauling the duffel
I packed.

Dre asks me if I
told my mother

about my plans
for the morning.

She must feel
how I get stiff

in her arms,
because she turns

on her night-light
to look at me.

"She deserves
the truth, Yaya.

I don't want to lie.
& you know

she's going to ask me."

Tears prick at my eyes.

Everyone spends
years, my entire

lifetime, lying to me
about my family,

but I'm the one
who supposedly

owes people the truth?

"Dre, I don't want
you to lie; just let me

get a head start.
I know it seems

unsafe, unkind, but
I do think it is

the right thing
for me to do."

She doesn't respond.
But she turns off the light

& holds me close
the whole night.

I kiss her gently
in the morning

when it's time
for me to leave.

———

Fifty Days After

At the airport I stand at the check-in line
trying not to draw attention.

I've done the research & because I'm
sixteen going on seventeen, I fly as an adult,

not an unaccompanied minor. The only hitch
is if they ask for my mother to sign a letter of consent.

But I heard this is hit-or-miss; it just depends
on the person checking you in.

I tried to get my ticket electronically, but it kept saying *error*.
I am not nervous. I am not nervous.

When the man at the desk calls me forward
I hand over my passport without saying a thing.

He looks at the picture, then at me. "You're underage.
Will you have a guardian with you?"

I shake my head no. He shakes his head sadly. "If you were
seventeen we could waive it. But as it is . . ."

Panic bubbles in my body. I can't not go. I can't not go.
I have to get on this flight.

I look the man at the desk straight in the eye.
He is youngish & seems new at his job.

I think of the best way to play this & decide to be up-front.
"I'm going to bury my father. My mother didn't know

I would need a guardian." I make myself sound confident.

I push the next words out. None of them are lies.

"My father was a passenger on flight 1112.
My father died on flight 1112. They're flying his body,

what is left of it, out today."

It's the first time I've said the words. Although reporters
have called the house & it was all over CNN

a few weeks ago, this is the first time I have said the words.
My father died on flight 1112.

For the rest of my life I will be known by that fact.
I wipe at my eyes with the heel of my hand.

The man at the desk blinks rapidly.
He squints down at my passport.

"Looks like you'll be seventeen soon. & really
the age restriction is more a recommendation than a
    requirement."

He hands me back my passport.
Prints out a ticket & circles my gate.

———————

CAMINO ✈ YAHAIRA

I start the sancocho
while Tía delivers a poultice
to a viejita with arthritis.

I brown the beef & chicken,
peel & chunk the yucca
& plantains.

This is the stew
we make for welcome,
& although I don't know

if I even want this girl here,
it seems the right thing to do.
I don't think about the money at the altar.

When Tía comes home,
I am chopping cilantro. Mashed
garlic sits in the mortar.

Usually when I cook
it's quick things:
pastelitos, bacalao with rice. Tostones.

But sancocho is a daylong dish to make.
It has many steps; it's making a pact with time
that you will be patient & the outcome will be delicious.

It is browning & boiling. Blending & straining.
It is meat & root vegetables. Herbs & salt.
It is hearty & made from the earth & heart.

Tía puts her bag away, turns on the kitchen radio.
Xiomara Fortuna's voice bellows out, & soon
we are both singing along.

If Tía suspects anything, she does not let on.
She cuts avocado & puts on a pot of rice.
She removes pulp from a chinola for juice.

Tía is a tight-lipped woman with few friends;
she says she only shares her secrets with the Saints,
her silence laid out like a dance floor for magic.

Yahaira is on the same flight as Papi's body.
I know exactly where she is in the air
without having to glance at a clock.

I've memorized this route
throughout my sixteen years. I don't check
my tablet. I don't worry about the plane.

Of course I worry about the plane.
I am sick with worry about a girl I don't know.
My hands shake as I wipe down the kitchen counter.

I should tell Tía. But I know if I do, she will call
Yahaira's mother. & I know if she does that,
her mother might learn about the money,

might learn what I've been planning.

I light a candle at Tía's altar & pray for safe passage
& that the crossroads be clear. & then with an hour left
of flight time, I make the phone call I've been dreading.

But sometimes a girl needs a favor.

———◆———

I spend the entire ride in Don Mateo's car
berating myself for agreeing
to this Yahaira's crazy plan.

My hands are sweating. & it's not because
the AC in Don Mateo's car doesn't work.
He was gruff as usual when he let me in the car

but I can tell even he's shaken by how eerily
familiar this all seems. Last time we did this
it seems like the world ended.

I told Don Mateo I need to receive my father's body,
not that I was picking up his other daughter.
I know he'd have told Tía immediately.

We are silent the entire ride. The closer we get
to the airport, the more I feel like I might throw up.
I try to distract myself with plans for Yahaira.

What am I going to do with a sister?
She'll have to sleep in my bed.
She'll probably have that gringa Spanish

& require me to translate for her.
She's probably a comparona who will expect
me to cook & clean.

Well, I will fling her back to the States
like a bat out of a cueva if she doesn't
act right. I should have never offered to help.

It is wrong, I know; my sister is not a comparona.
She seems kind, & thoughtful. The pain in her eyes
is a twin for the ache in mine.

I am so afraid of liking her.
Of wanting her to be my family.
My heart cannot afford any more relatives.

I realize too late I've bitten off half the polish on my thumbnail.
Now my manicure looks like un relajo.
I try to bite the rest of the polish off

so at least my nails will match. But it was a stupid reflex;
now I have five fucked-up nails instead of one.
Don Mateo pulls the car up to the terminal,

but I can't get out. I reach for the handle, but
it's like my hand gets stuck there. I can hear my breath
shudder in & out of my body, loud in my ears.

"I can take you back home, Camino.
It's okay if I'm a little late for work.
I'm sure the officials will understand."

I shake my head & roll my shoulders.
I've faced worse things than an airport.
I've survived worse things than are behind those doors.

"Thank you, Don Mateo. I'll be okay."
He raises his bushy eyebrows & pats me
softly on the arm.

When I'm at the airport entryway
I stop completely still. My feet feel stuck.
The last time I was here. The last time I was here

was not so long ago. It was a day just like today.
It was the day that changed everything.
I am not sure if I can go inside.

———

Although I brace myself, I am not ready
for the wave of grief
that smacks me in the face

as I enter through the airport doors.
I immediately find the screen with information.
The plane should be landing in twenty minutes.

The information is right there,
with a gate number & everything.
There is an excited crowd of folks waiting for family,

but none of them are crying. There is no one weeping,
no loud upset yelling. The excitement & love & anxiety
is like a breathing being in the terminal.

I feel like I am trying to reconcile two very
different pictures. My heart wants to make them whole,
but my brain knows my father will not walk through those doors;

my brain does not know if my sister will.
What if something happens? Takeoff & landing
are the most dangerous parts of flight.

Ugh! I want to smack myself for even thinking it—
I watch the monitor, counting down the minutes
until descent. It feels closer to twenty hours.

& then the board clears. No new information.
My hands begin to shake, my breathing uneven.
Did something go wrong? Did something happen?

I grab a man in an airport uniform, but I can't get out the words
to ask him. I simply point up at the board. His annoyance
shifts & he gently pats my hand; he must understand

what I haven't said. "It landed just fine. I think they
are simply trying to update the arrival gate.
A breath I didn't know I'd bitten whooshes through my teeth.

Before I know it, people trickle out of customs.

Everything seems so normal, so unlike six weeks ago.
They've all moved on. Or were never moved
in the first place.

People in business suits holding briefcases.
Tall, shapely women in high heels
& bedazzled jeans, grand-looking doñas

with mahogany canes & skirt suits.

& finally a beautiful girl, with tight curls:
A morenita with a pink duffel in her hand
looking pensive & determined.

It is almost as if she does not imagine
there will be anyone there waiting for her.
Her eyes do a sweep of the people

but pass right by me. A second later she looks back.
Tears fill my eyes. I stare at the ceiling lights
until the sting recedes.

When I look back down she is standing before me.

———•———

YAHAIRA & CAMINO

I was never afraid of flying in the past.

But today, the rise of the plane made my stomach plunge.
I had a middle seat, & the woman beside me

kept the window shade open the entire time.
I peeked once & saw the huge blue ocean below us.

I kept my eyes shut completely after that.
Even when the flight attendant asked if I wanted juice.

Even when the man next to me farted loudly.
Even when the pilot said we were descending.

& there was a moment when the wheels first touched down
that my heart plummeted in my chest, but then we were slowing

& a smattering of passengers erupted into applause.
The old lady in the seat beside me said in Spanish,

"They don't do that as much anymore. This must be a plane
of Dominicans returning home;

when you touch down on this soil, you must clap when you land.
Para dar gracias a dios. Regrezamos." & I smiled back.

———

Although I've flown
in the States for different

tournaments, this is my first time
in another country.

In the airport, the messages
are bilingual.

The customs line is long,
& I scan the form I filled out on the plane

with all my information.
I pay ten dollars for a tourist card &

am afraid I will be rejected.
I answer all the customs agent's

questions about where I am staying
& why I am here.

Her hard eyes soften a bit
when I mention my father's funeral.

She scans my passport
& then I am walking through the doors

here. I am here. I am here.
& then I see, that so is she.

Camino reaches up & touches my cheek.
"Te pareces igualito a él."

& it's true I've always favored my father.
But so does she. In real life, it's not quite like looking into a
    mirror.

Her eyes are light, a hazel color, her lashes long.
She is supermodel thin where I am curvier,

& for a moment I want to smack her hard.
For wearing my face. For looking like

a Yahaira-lite version of me.

For so clearly being my father's daughter.
& then guilt swamps over me. I am the one he left her for.

She said on video chat he called her "India linda."
& I wonder what he saw when he looked at her.

Her eyes fill, but I know she won't cry. She seems like
the kind of girl who can will her eyes to unmake tears.

"You look just like him. Except your eyes.
Papi never knew how to hide what he felt,

but you know how to draw down window shades."
& I know she means that all the anger I feel

is locked inside. That I am blank-faced.
The way I was at the chessboard.

"*We* look just like him.
You must have gotten your coloring from your mother."

She nods & sucks in a deep breath,
the mention of her mother wiping the softness from her face.

She drops her hand. We both take a step back.

———◆———

Without my asking, Camino takes my duffel in hand
& swings it onto her shoulder.

We leave the coolness of the air-conditioning
& I'm immediately swarmed

by a heavy humidity & a flurry of movement.
All around me people in slacks & colorful dresses hug,

babies cling to their mothers' legs, & other teens in shorts
& caps walk around selling Chiclets gum, green mints.

Camino weaves with ease by crying couples & parents
toward a slim man leaning against a broke-down car.

He has the kind of smile that would have made
Papi fidget with his big gold ring.

The same ring he said he would plant in the face
of any man who messed with his daughter.

In other words, he looks like trouble. I don't smile back.
& instead stop in my tracks. "Is this our taxi?"

Camino shrugs. "The unofficial ones tend to be cheaper."
I shake my head at her & weave back toward the taxi line.

The one with marked & labeled cars,
where an old man with a kind smile helps us with my bag

& holds the door open as we climb in.
Camino's mouth is in a hard line.

I stare at the window as we drive & try
to ask Camino about the scenery.

She smirks at my Spanish
& responds to me in English.

I hope my face does not show surprise
at her vocabulary & accent:

I mean, she sounds like an English professor, with her
perfect pronunciations, but she must have worked hard

to speak so fluently. My Spanish
is nowhere near as good, & it's my first language.

I feel like I am losing to my sister   & it's only the opening.

———————

The cabdriver slows the car in front of
an aqua house with a fenced-in front porch.

Before Camino can reach into her wallet
I thrust some dollar bills at the driver.

I'm hoping this will make Camino feel better;
I don't need her to pay. But instead

she makes a sound low in her throat
& hops out the car without a word.

It seems my money offends her.

There is a woman hunched over a side garden
pulling up some greens by the roots.

I cannot imagine my father in this
little, cozy house.

He was a man who loved his luxuries.
& this is a barrio house.

A nice barrio house, but a barrio
nonetheless: stray dogs walking the streets,

garbage piling into the gutters.
Mud stretching up the stone walls enclosing the casita.

My father would have hated
getting his freshly waxed shoes dirty.

The tiny woman by the garden straightens up,
& when she glances at me, all the herbs she'd been picking

fall from her hand. She is staring, at me, I think,
until I realize she is staring beyond me.

"Camino, muchacha del carajo, what have you done?"

Camino's Tía Solana's body shakes as she hugs me.
& I lean into the arms & warmth of this woman who is a stranger.

I want to ask her so many questions
but her eyes are wet when she pulls back,

& I realize I want to fight her
for what are actually my father's sins.

"Where is your mother, niña?"
I glance at Camino, who indicates with a shrug

that I am entirely on my own. I rub my earlobe.
Camino's Tía takes a hard look at her before

she guides me into the house as if I am a fragile old woman.
She seats me at the small round table in the living room.

She sets a bowl of sancocho before me, with a plate of concón.
"Tell me the whole story,

but first eat what your sister made for you."

———

I am helping Camino pick herbs for tea,
the act of picking the fresh leaves reminding me of Dre.

The mangy dog that sits outside the gate sniffs
the metal bars from where he sits. Camino opens it for him,

& he settles quietly into a patch of weeds.
"Does the dog follow you everywhere?" I ask her.

I do not tell her Papi did not let us have a dog,
despite how much I begged or even as Mami argued it'd be
        good for me.

"No, Vira Lata doesn't really leave his spot near the house.
He won't go that way." She gestures to the right.

"It leads to a busy street. He got hit by a car once,
& I think it made him shy of too many vehicles.

He likes it here because the neighborhood kids
leave him scraps, & Tía's little fruit trees offer shade.

The man next door, Don Mateo, built a little doghouse
on raised legs for him to climb into if the water rises."

But I notice that when Camino goes to close the gate,
& it seems she's turning left, the dog stands at alert,

wagging his short stub tail.
Camino catches my raised brow & laughs.

"Oh yes, if I'm going in that direction, he sometimes follows;
he loves the beach. He likes to chase

the salty air as I swim. When we are riled up,
the beach soothes us both, doesn't it, Latita?"

She is gentle with the dog. & I have to look away from the
      tenderness.
Through the gate I see a tall man standing across the street,

but what brings goose bumps to my skin
is the way he's watching Camino,

like he wishes he were the dog beneath her hand,
like he would love to sink his teeth into her.

I turn to point him out,
but by the time she follows my whispered words

& pointed finger,
the man is already gone.

The night is not over before the house phone rings.
Yahaira & Tía sit on the couch like old girlfriends,
& I know my "Aló?" is laced with salt.

A woman speaks rapidly & I only catch
that she wants to speak to Yahaira.
She sounds exactly how I imagined

my father's other woman to sound:

high maintenance, demanding. Una chica
plástica all the way through.
I pass the cordless phone & Yahaira raises a brow.

The woman is yelling before she gets the receiver
up to her ear. Tía pats Yahaira softly on her back
& I just can't. This girl needs no sympathy.

At least she has a mother. At least she has choices.
She has been well fed her whole life. She is clearly loved.
I bet you no one ever forgot her birthday.

& given the burial plans & Yahaira's arrival,
I'm sure Tía has forgotten that in a few days
it will be mine. I try & fight back the bitterness.

I know I know better.

But it also feels like my life is a careening motoconcho

on a rain-slick road   rushing   rushing toward

something bigger & madder.

———

Fifty-One Days After

Mami is on her way to DR
tomorrow, & she is pissed.

Apparently she knocked on the Johnsons' door, panicked,
thinking something had happened,

& when Dr. Johnson asked Dre,
she stayed quiet for as long as she could

before she broke down & told the truth.
Honestly, I'm surprised Dre waited

that long. That she didn't call Mami
as soon as my plane took off.

Maybe she realizes there are other
shades besides black & white.

But even as Mami yells at me over the phone,
all I can feel is the sweetest relief.

No one can force me to go back home.

The funeral is in three days,
after the remains are cleared at customs

& delivered here to this house.
Three days to figure out my sister,

my father,   myself.

———

Do you believe
in ghosts?

What kind
of question
is that?

I don't know . . .
it's just that—

Of *course* I believe in ghosts.
There are spirits
everywhere.

You
for real?

Anyone
who says otherwise
es un come mierda.

Mami doesn't
believe in ghosts.

Maybe you don't
have them
in New York City.

So, you think Papi's ghost
will live in DR?

I think his ghost
will live
wherever we carry him.

Can a ghost be
in two places at once?

Definitely:
if it's
Papi's ghost.

Papi's ghost would have had
a lot of practice.

———

Fifty-Two Days After

It has been a whole day
where I wait for Mami to arrive

& get to know my sister's aunt
who insists I call her my aunt—

& watch my sister pretend
she isn't watching me.

Nothing is familiar.

Not the whirring ceiling fan,
or the loud generator.

Not the neighbors who keep coming by
to hug Camino & reminisce about Papi.

The Dominican Republic
is like everything I imagined

& beyond anything
I could have pictured.

I am awakened from the bed
I share with Camino

by a fruit-cart guy yelling
mango aguacate tomate.

On the porch,
when I'm rocking in the chair

I watch little pink & green
salamanders run up the blue walls.

I have never seen so much color,
every house its own watercolor painting.

The papaya Tía Solana cuts for breakfast
is tender between my teeth.

I take picture after picture on my phone,
sending everything to Dre.

I cannot imagine having grown up here.
Cannot understand how my father

flipped himself back & forth.

———◆———

Tía Solana tells Camino she should show me her beach,
& Camino flinches as if someone raised a hand to hit her.

I pretend not to notice, but she must see the way my face falls
because when Tía Solana turns her back, Camino leans to me.

"The beach isn't safe. There's this guy who hangs out there;
I don't think he would be very nice for either of us to see."

It is the first time I've seen Camino be anything but sure,
the way she bites on her lower lip & won't look me in the eye.

I think I know what kind of guy Camino must be describing,
& I tell her so. How we have disrespectful dudes in NYC, too.

As soon as the words are out of my mouth,
Camino moves away from me,

making a noise of disgust deep in her throat.
"You think you know so much, Yahaira.

But what you know wouldn't sweeten
a cup of tea." She huffs off toward the patio,

& I wonder what she means & where she learned to judge
so harshly someone she barely just met.

———————

I know
I was harder on Yahaira
than I should have been.

But she shows up
after I've lived a whole life
& wants to pretend

we have so much in common?
She can't possibly have known
anyone, or any situation, like El Cero.

She has no idea what it means
to completely abandon your dreams.
She cannot.

Because it seems
what everyone has known but me
is that I won't be a doctor.

I won't ever be anything more
than a girl from a small barrio
who helps her aunt with herbs.

& that might be the whole of my life.
& that will have to be enough.
Isn't that what makes a dream a dream?

You wake up eventually.
But that girl, that girl gets to keep
living in the clouds.

———

When Mami pulls up to the house
driving a tiny Prius, the first thing I notice

is how hard her hands are clutching
the steering wheel.

I did not even know Mami had a license,
much less that she would use it.

I try not to flinch & grab Camino
although I'm nervous.

Mami gets out of the car with only a purse,
but I see a suitcase in the back—

she rushes out the car, leaving
the driver's door open.

She runs to me,
pulls me into a tight tight hug.

& I know I scared her.
I wish I could tell her that I scared myself.

Beside me, Camino is unmoving,
as if made of marble.

My mother steps back from me &
runs hands down her jeans.

She kisses Camino's aunt hello,
& I realized then, they would have met before.

Ma was Camino's mother's friend;
she's probably even been to this house.

Theirs is an awkward greeting. & then she takes
a long hard look at Camino. & I can see in her eyes

that she sees how much we look alike;
this girl who could have sprung from her body,

how much we look like Papi,
both of us looking like we could have sprung from his.

She takes a deep breath. So do I.
I do not know how Mami will greet Camino.

I do not know what she is feeling in this moment.
I want to make the moment easy but don't know how.

Mami takes the decision from me.

She leans in & kisses the air near Camino's cheek:
"It's nice to meet you, Camino.

I know you don't know me, & it's small consolation,
but your father loved you very much."

———————

Mami & Tía Solana sit inside the little house.
Camino & I rock in the chairs on the tiny porch.

It's strange to be outside but still be barred in.
The wicker rocking chair bites into my thighs.

The stars overhead are scattered rhinestones
glued onto the night's deep, dark fabric.

Camino passes me a cigar she's been smoking.
I take a small puff & immediately start coughing.

She laughs & roughly rubs circles on my back.
That thing does *not* taste as good as it smells.

"Just breathe, Yaya. It'll ease up."
& from somewhere I didn't know existed,

the phrase spells itself in smoke, in Papi's voice.
Just breathe, negra, just breathe.

Pain yawns open inside my chest,
a wail pulls up from my mouth.

The sob barreling past my lips,
& pulling an army of tears with it. I can't stop.

My body heaves in the rocking chair.
& Camino rubs my back in small, small circles.

"Just breathe, Yaya. Así."
& through the screen of my tears

I see her own eyes are full, ready to cry,
but maybe I'm just imagining it.

———•———

I have never been an older sister to anyone.
I didn't even grow up with one of the strays.
The chickens we killed were for food & ceremonies,

& I didn't name or coddle even one of them.
So it is a strange feeling that's being tattooed on my heart.
This need to comfort my crying, sad sister.

What do I know about providing comfort?
Of making myself a place of solace?
& yet it seems I know a lot because Yaya

folds herself into my arms & wets my blouse
with her sniffles, & I don't even want to smack her
across the back of her head for ruining one of my good shirts.

———

Fifty-Three Days After

Camino & I walk a long ways to a river the next day.
& I wonder at how our father split himself & his love

& implanted us each with something of him
because the girl swims like a dolphin while I plop

around in the water, holding on to big rocks & kicking my feet.
& I feel competitive for a second, want to tell Camino

I would dust her on the chessboard if she played.
But I know this is petty. Swimming seems like therapy

to Camino. Her shoulders drop; her skin glows.
It is the closest to happy I've seen her since getting here.

On the other hand, chess has never been stress relief for me;
chess is the definition of stress itself. My mind wrestling

with every possibility & outcome, my thumb war with the pieces
trying to decide where they should land does not seem half as
    smooth

as Camino's backstroke. I push onto my back & float
downstream. It is hard to remind myself I am not playing

against my sister. We are on the same team, I tell myself.
Even if I don't actually believe that.

———

Fifty-Four Days After

The ceremony we had for Papi in New York
is nothing compared to what is planned in DR.

Tía & Camino arrange an entire party.
Mami looks on disapprovingly

as a band of men in white show up with drums
& tambourines, & it's a good thing the grave site

isn't too far from the church because dozens
& dozens of people show up, until we're a blur,

a smudge of people dressed like ash
advancing down the street.

I borrowed a light-colored dress from Camino,
& we walk down the street arm in arm.

People sing songs I don't know.
I think Papi would have loved us making such a fuss.

———

at the grave site
the casket is lowered

the earth again
welcoming
a song home

Mami heaves
as if she will jump in

the caoba trees
bow low
the wood gleams

words intoned
I lick sweat off my lip

Tía rocks
back & forth
I cannot hold her

my sister
grasps my hand

I feel her squeeze
& do not let go
hold tight

the ground
ruptured

my father's
body
fills the hole

dirt is thrown
on the casket

filled up
& made whole
again

but not the same

———

Tía Solana begins the novena, the nine days of prayer,
immediately after the body is lowered into the ground.

Mami sits in a corner of the house. Not praying. Not moving.
Tears steadily fall down her cheeks

but not a single sob pushes forth from her mouth.
I touch her shoulder once, but she is holding vigil.

I can't imagine how difficult it must be for her
to be here. All the painful memories she must have,

all the ones she will have after today. I try not to feel
guilt for having made her face this. But it still twists

me up to see how hard it is for her to look at this house,
to speak to these neighbors, to imagine this life my father had.

People come from all over to feast on the food
we spent yesterday cooking; to pull rosary beads

through their fingers & usher my father's spirit
into heaven. & I wonder where his spirit

has been this whole time if only now is when
we are all officially praying for him?

Has he been here? Has he been here this whole time?
Has he watched us wrestle with the gift & curse he left behind?

After the novena,
all the neighbors
fill plates of food.

Everyone but Yahaira's
mami eats. She
sits by the window

staring at absolutely
nothing. Even Vira
Lata is chewing a bone

out back. I walk over
to her, but stop before I speak.
I know I am hovering.

I am so unsure of myself
around this woman.
Who probably wishes

I had never been born.
As if she hears my thought,
she turns & pins me with her gaze.

"I noticed you were rubbing
a hand on your chest,
& Yahaira told me you've lost weight," I say.

Her eyes fly to her daughter,
who is listening to old Juanita
tell one of her elaborate stories.

I force myself to rush on.
I don't want to seem like
I'm sucking up to her.

It's just so clear she's in pain.
It hurts me to watch it. It
reminds me of my own.

"It's just, all studies show
these are signs of high stress.
The aches. The loss of appetite.

Anyway, I fixed you a plate.
You should try & sleep tonight.
& remind yourself to take deep breaths."

I wait. I know my tone
is a presumptuous one
she will berate me for.

Instead, she reaches out
& takes the plate I offer.
A soft smile tugs at her lips.

"He always did say
you would make a
wonderful doctor.

He had grand plans that you'd
attend Columbia. He said once
you were in the States, he wanted you close.

We live right by the school,
you know?" & I don't know
who is more surprised,

me at the future my
father imagined without my knowing,
or her, at the disclosure.

I nod & walk away
before either one of us
says more. It seems

we've arrived
at peaceful ground,
& I want her to have

this memory
when it is all
said & done.

You should stop smoking those cigars.
Where did you get it anyway?

                                        Tía uses them
                                      in her ceremonies
                    & always has some stashed in the house.

Ceremonies?
What ceremonies?

                    Oh, girl, you got a lot to learn
                        about this side of the family.
              Did you ever wonder about Papi's beads?

He didn't wear jewelry
except his ring.

                        It was like he was two
                    completely different men.
                It's like he split himself in half.

It's like he bridged himself
across the Atlantic.

                    Never fully here nor there.
                    One toe in each country.

          Ni aquí ni allá.

———

By the time the vecinos leave,
it is after eleven.

Mami goes to wash up, mumbling
about sleeping in a house her husband

once shared with another woman.
She wanted to stay in a hotel, but I refused to leave.

& she refused to leave me.
Camino & I are on the patio,

sitting in the rocking chairs just as Camino comments
that storm clouds are gathering.

It is then that Tía Solana comes over

& gives Camino a long, long hug.
"Lo siento that this

is how you spent your birthday."
I feel lightning-struck dumb.

"Today is your birthday?
Why would you plan a burial today?"

Camino shrugs
& leans into Tía's petting hand.

I can't believe I'm empty-handed
for my sister's birthday.

I go into the bedroom Camino is sharing with me
& rummage through my suitcase.

I have a pack of gum, some hair
product she might like, my travel documents,

Papi's papers that Camino might want one day,
but nothing I can gift.

———•———

At midnight it will be the end of my birthday
& the day that Papi is put into the ground.
Yahaira's eyes are swollen from crying

& I can tell she is worried
that our relationship will be another thing
we need to mourn & bury.

Sometimes, I look at her & it hits me
that she is the only person who can understand what I feel,
but she is also at the root of the hurt I'm feeling.

Her mother barely looked at me the whole day,
& I know I'll have to go through with my plan.
I am seventeen today.

Yahaira tells me she is going to sleep.
Her mother & Tia have already retired
to the room they are sharing.

Her mother looked bewildered all day,
like a gallo who slept through the morning.
But before she goes to bed she reminds Yahaira

she bought plane tickets for them to depart in three days.
I think about the leaving: how my sister was left money.
How my father's wife was left with a valid marriage certificate.

& in a few days' time,
how they will both try to leave me.
It is a tiring thing to have to continue forgiving a father

who is no longer here.

———

I go inside. I have a feeling Camino wants to be alone.
In the living room I stop still at the altar.

Mami & I have been ignoring the altar in the corner.
I don't know much about Saints or ancestors, only the rumors

of sacrificing chickens & how it all relates to voodoo.
I don't even know if that's what this is.

Camino called it something else,
& says the prayers & sacrifices

are important to having a relationship with the Saints,
having a relationship with those who sweep the way,

nudge open the doors for us to walk forward,
for us to walk through.

Camino or Tía has placed a small offering of rum &
coconut chunks, roasted corn on a small plate.

I can't imagine my father kneeling
or praying at the foot of this altar. & yet,

I think about the silver coin he always carried in his pocket
& how its twin sits on the altar here.

I think about how he would always say something
about San Anthony, & isn't that the statue by the door?

My father hid this part of himself tight inside his pockets,
but it still slipped through the stitching   I just never paid
     attention.

I carefully pick up the frame with his picture, lift the candle.
Mami has decided we will return home in three days.

Taped to the back of Papi's frame is an envelope of money.
I wonder if this is the cash I sent last week. Is this what Camino

is to survive off of?

———————

In the bedroom we are sharing,
moonlight peeks through the gathering storm clouds,
& for a second its light glows on Yahaira's dark face.

I look at how beautiful she is, my almost twin.
I feel like a fish Tía buys from el mercado: gutted.
My spine pulled out from my back.

When I am sure Yahaira is snoring softly,
I reach into her duffel bag. Searching.
But before I find what I want,

there, at the bottom, a marriage certificate.
One with my mother's name on it. Dated
after both Yahaira & I were born.

Her family was always first.
The real one that I merely interrupted.
I want to crumple to the floor. I want to crumple the page.

Instead, I rip it up.

All the stupid things my father did but never said.
All these secrets & mysteries he kept.
All these papers, papers, papers.

Maybe I can fold these jagged scraps
into a yola that will sail me across the Atlantic.
Maybe I can string these dozens of words into a rope

I can use to zip-line to the States. I can't pay tuition,
or light bills,   or El Cero   with an old man's regrets.
There goes the last thing I had of him.

I grab what I originally wanted   & leave.

—————

I wake up. I am alone. & although nothing
has shifted in the night, something feels off.

Outside, the patter of rain lands against wet earth
& I want to let it lull me to sleep but I get up.

I can't shake the feeling of wrongness. On the floor,
half buried beneath the bed, is the ripped-up certificate

of marriage I brought with me.
I thought Camino might have wanted it.

It *was* at the bottom of my bag.

I realize I don't know my sister at all.

If this was Dre I would know how to
wrap my arms around her & hug the mad away.

If this was a newbie who lost a game
I would know what piece of wisdom

I need to offer. But it's Camino.

I know if I were her,
this would not have been

what I was searching for.

———

I am quiet as I leave the house.
Holding back tears.
It's been clear to me since the beginning

how it is that this must end.
The quickly scrawled note
I wrote for Tía is on the altar,

the first place I know she will turn
for solace when she realizes
that I am gone.

It is the middle of the night,
too early to make my way
to begin walking the four miles.

Vira Lata whines at my heels,
& I scratch him softly behind an ear.
There is one last place I have to see

before I go.

———◆———

I am not dressed for travel.
When I arrive at the airport in the morning
I know I will call attention:

no suitcase, no backpack, no guardian.
I only have my purse, the money,
& the gift Yahaira does not know she's given to me.

I will have to bribe someone to buy me the ticket;
I will need to bribe someone to pretend to be my
parent. I will say the person is an aunt or uncle,

I will explain my parents are dead.
It's possible I might be pulled aside if the agent decides
to ask extra questions. I don't try to think that far.

I am certainly not dressed for the beach
in my sneakers & long jeans,
my hair bunned up tight to look like my sister's.

But I have to come here
to the water's edge.
To the sand that has always hugged me close.

My mother stood with me here,
& looked outward as she would tell me to wave
at my father.

It was here my mother would bring me
to lay out a blanket as we made a meal
of soft bread & hard cheese.

This stretch of boundless land
was where she would hold my hands
& we would dance to the live music

coming from the resort next door.
I am crying before I know it.
When the sun comes up I must be hard-eyed

but in the glint of night
I say goodbye to my mother,
to my mother country,

as the rain begins to fall.

———————

A rustling in the branches
makes the hairs on my neck stand.
No.   No.   No.

How did he know I was here?
How does he always know I'm here?
He must have been watching   all this time.

"Your sister, she looks just like you.
But has American written all over her.
I wonder if I can make her acquaintance?"

I ignore him & take a step beyond his reach.
Vira Lata at my feet growls low in his throat.
The rain does not feel quite as gentle as it did.

I tell myself the rain is the reason
I'm shaking. & not the threat to Yahaira.
& not El Cero here. Crowding my last hours.

I can imagine what he sees in me:
a trembling girl in sneakers & denim.
Inside the purse I hold tight at my side

is the only key to freedom I own.
That, a small kit of makeup,
& Yahaira's passport.

The rest I left behind with a note.
Money for Tía & Carline.
An explanation of the need to leave.

El Cero brushes closer, & I tighten my grip on the purse.
He's asking me a question but his voice seems far away.
I don't want him to know how much I'm carrying

but maybe I can ease this situation.
"I have money. I'll pay you what my father owed.
Half now & half tomorrow? Let it be settled."

I don't want to make him angry.
I want to guard my secrets close.
I take a step back to move away from him.

He rubs a thumb across his bottom lip.
"I don't know. I've had plans for you.
But maybe the money would be enough.

He owed me two thousand dollars
for this upcoming year." I fiddle with
the strap of my purse, & he raises a brow.

"Don't tell me, Camino,
you are walking around with
that kind of cash?"

My hands shake in the bag
as I try to figure out the right number
of bills to get me out of here.

My heart is racing in my chest.
I grab what I think is enough
& shove it at him.

"Here. This should cover half."
I calculate quickly how much
I'll have to cut back on to make my new amount stretch.

I begin edging back toward the tree,
ready to make a run for it,
but El Cero's hand grabs my sleeve.

He stares down at the dollars
like they are a crossword puzzle
with the clue in a language he doesn't know.

"Why do you have this much cash?
Were you meeting someone else out here?
Why are you clutching your bag? Is there more?"

His strong grasp yanks at the bag
& despite my tight grip
he is bigger & stronger, & he wrenches it from me.

He runs his hand through my bag,
pulling out the embossed gold of the passport,
the stark white of the envelope

that holds my entire future.

"Why, Caminito? It seems you
were trying to make a run for it?
Without paying a debt. Tsk, tsk."

I try to grab the passport & money,
but he holds both high above his head
like this is all a game, a middle-school tiff.

Vira Lata must feel my distress
because now he lets out a long bark
before he races off into the trees.

"Camino   Camino   figured it out somehow.
Tried to get away without making a payment.
Tried to get away without saying goodbye."

The storm clouds overhead
cover the moon completely.
Thunder sounds in the distance, &

I wipe furiously at water on my face.
The tides will rise quickly.
But not as quick as my anger.

"You're such a fucking dirt bag.
Un grosero, not worthy to bite the flea
that bites a stray.

I don't know what converted you
into this monster.
But I bet your sister is turning in her grave."

The words come out in a fast whoosh
but do not sound like me.
When the lightning flashes, I see El Cero's face

has twisted into an ugly mask.
He grabs me by my blouse,
pulling me up to my tippy toes;

spittle flies out his mouth
as he yells directly into my face.
"Do not ever mention her,

you uppity, ugly bitch."
& when he shoves me back,
my foot twists painfully beneath me.

Above me El Cero puts the money &
my passport—Yahaira's passport—
into his back pocket.

———

As the thunder rumbles,
I gather up the torn-up pieces of the marriage certificate.

I can tell from the stillness in the house, Camino isn't here.
I don't know the rules of sisterhood.

Am I supposed to try to find her?
Am I supposed to leave her alone?

The thought that she might be alone & angry
on a night she should be celebrating her birthday

makes me stand up & walk into the living room. Stare at the
   altar.
Papi, if you can hear me, help us both. For once.

A folded-up envelope with Tía's name
rests on the altar. I don't remember it being there before.

Outside, the frantic barking of the mutt
                    grabs my attention.

He sounds as if someone is trying to attack him,
but when I peek through the curtains I see he's barking at the
   house.

I can't help the feeling that my sister needs me.
& for the first time in my life I am actually here to help.

As I turn to grab my phone to see if I can find her,
I bang into a standing lamp that topples over.

From the bedroom they are sharing,
I hear shuffling & then Mami & Tía

rush through the doorway.
But Tía's brown face goes completely pale.

She clutches a hand to her throat.
"¿Y mi Camino? ¿Adónde está Camino?"

———————

the earth spins
round & round
like palo dance

a trance. Advance
across, the mud,
zoom

zoom into tree
skin a match
I want to detach

from me

      a man laughs
      am I laughing?
he kneels in the dirt beside me.

stomach sick
crawling
skin   slick

push away
kick him back
scratch at the eyes

mouth   open
cry   cry   cry
for help

Tía is shaking
as I guide her to a chair.

Mami pours her
a glass of water.

I've seen enough crime shows
to know we need to try & narrow

down where Camino
might have gone.

"I sent her money.
A few days ago."

Mami gasps
but is otherwise silent.

"Would she have
left for the capital?" I ask Tía.

But Tía dismisses that with a hand.
"We have no family there."

Although I feel like I'm betraying her
I offer, "My passport is missing."

At this, Mami pushes up to her feet.
"She would pass herself off as you.

Solana, we need to go to the airport."

But Tía shakes her head again.
"It doesn't open until four a.m.

The girl is impetuous,
but she wouldn't walk the roads

at this time of night;
she would wait for the sun.

Maybe her friend Carline.
She might go to her."

But this time it's me
who is disbelieving.

"She loves on her best friend
like a favorite doll. Treats her fragile-like.

She wouldn't wake her.
She wouldn't make her complicit."

The three of us stare at one another.
Until we hear the whine right outside the door.

The dog must have found his way
underneath the fence.

Tía & I catch eyes
at the exact same time.

There is only one place
Camino would go.

———

Mami pulls the car up as far as she can
but I am out the door before she even stops;

running through the trees toward the water,
I hear a low moan   like someone in pain.

As the trees clear,
I see Camino on the ground thrashing against

a man who kneels above her;
she's kicking him in the stomach as he tries to hold her still.

The sky has opened up;
rain drips down her face.

They have not seen me yet.

It is the first time I am glad to be taller & thicker
than Camino as I rush out &

run up behind them, shoving the man hard
so that he falls into the sand.

He angles his shoulder, & I can tell
he wants to bum-rush me.

I crouch down to cover Camino's hunched
& trembling body. She clumsily clings to my waist.

Her blouse is ripped open.
& like the dog frantically barking beside us,

I bare my teeth at the man.

"You've been her sister for what, two days?
You're going to want to mind your business."

I ball my fists the way Papi taught me, thumbs outside.
"You'll want to leave Camino alone from now on."

His face contorts in anger.
He charges at me, but headlights flood the darkness.

———————

My mother's face peeks from the trees
as Tía Solana jumps out into the clearing,

her huge machete glinting in her hand.
I trust she knows exactly how to swing it.

The man takes a step back,
tries to fix his face into something more innocent.

He's going to try to lie his way out of this,
I can tell.

Even with the rain, the distant sound of lightning,
I can hear Tía praying, her soft voice undercutting all the noise.

She comes & stands by my side,
murmuring under her breath.

I bend down to help Camino to her feet.
Hold her to me with an arm around her waist.

Camino is uncharacteristically quiet.
I want to whisper in her ear,

"I know, I know. I know this fear. You're okay.
I'm here. I got you."

& the feeling is so clear it chokes me up
so much I can't actually say the words.

The lights cut out from the car,
& Mami steps from the vehicle.

She doesn't carry a single weapon,
nothing but her cell phone & the rolitos in her hair.

But you would think she was armed to the teeth
the way she pulls her shoulders back,

& there in her bearing, you see
she is a general's daughter.

She looks this man straight in the face.

"This girl does not exist for you anymore.
She doesn't live here. You won't be able to reach her."

Tía's praying gets louder, & she smacks the machete
hard against her open palm. Behind me Camino whimpers.

Off the ocean air, wind is starting to churn faster.
It smacks at the collar of the man's shirt.

Tía's praying is now at full volume, words I don't know,
but   I do know. I feel them in my chest.

It's as if she's silenced the night, everything
but the wind, & the wind has its own voice,

& it has joined with ours. It buffets at the man's hair
& clothing. & we are here: Tía like a bishop,

slashing her long machete. Mami, the knight with rims. My body
in front of my sister's body: queens.

Papi, who I know is here too. He did
build that castle he always promised.

Even the wind, & rain, & night:
even the light: has come to our side.

We stand for her. For each other.
With clenched fists & hard jaw—

We will protect Camino at all costs.
We will protect one another.

The man reaches into his back pocket,
& I feel the fear in Camino's body.

But Mami cuts through it with her hard words.
"You don't want to mess with me.

I am not a nobody. There is nowhere you can run
where my family would not find you.

Don't even think about it."
Beside me Camino finds her voice.

"Give me back what you took. All of it."

& when Tía hisses through her teeth
the man throws a packet onto the sand.

Keeping Camino behind me, I bend to pick it up.
I don't know what convinced him:

Mami's confident belief in who she is
& her own power, Tía's clear determination

to kill the man if she must, or just the belief
that none of this is worth it.

We stand there. Camino is crying into my back,
& I'm shaking where I hug the arms

she's wrapped around my waist.
The moment he turns his back on us,

Mami's face fills with relief.
She presses a trembling hand to her mouth

before she shoos at me to get to the car.
Only Tía is unmoving, unflinching as she

stares at the man walking toward the resort lights.
I worry for a second that she might chase him down,

but as if I said it out loud, she looks at me & winks.
"Everyone gets what they deserve eventually, mi'ja."

With glints in our eyes, dressed for dreaming,
we walk back to the car.

———

I hold on
    to the person
the one

who came
    to take me
when I look

at her I see lights
    a bright blue glow
from behind her

I hear a humming
    as if coming
from the wind itself

or as if the clouds
    swirl inside me
calling on me

to breathe
    a purple black red
burgundy light

caresses my face
    they are here
to take me

they are here
    I press myself closer
to   Yahaira? & behind her

the blue light becomes
    a woman, dressed in larimar.
Sharp knife in hand,

she smiles   all teeth.
    The humming quiets,
Tía, I realize, Tía's voice

has called the Saints.
    Tía's voice has come
to take me

all these women
    here to take me
home.

———

At the house I help Camino out
of her torn top. I try & reach for her jeans

but it only forces her to cry harder.
So I slip her shoes off & help her sit on the bed.

I run to the bathroom to grab a towel
I use to wipe the mud off her feet.

The moment she lies on her back
she rolls to throw up on the floor.

"Shock," Tía says. "Who knows how long
she was in the rain trying to think how to get away."

Tía boils a cup of tea. Sits gently next to Camino,
gives her small sips as she pets her hair.

I want to help Tía but have no idea what to do.
& so I climb into bed beside Camino, on her other side,

tuck my chin into her shoulder.
Throw my arm around her middle.

Let her know   she is safe.

———◆———

I am in between dreams
in one dream Yahaira
wraps around me

like one of those strangler figs.
I imagine she is that tree
absorbing me   I want to tell her

I am sorry   I want to tell her
she is welcome   but
before I get the words out

I wake up in another dream
in this one Tía has her face
close to my face

her face is covered in tears
I smell her warm scent of
chamomile & honey

feel her hands on my cheek
I am hers I am hers I am hers
she says & she is right

I dream my father
sits on the corner of the bed
his weight

                    on the mattress

                                              on my heart

his head in his hands

he looks like an old man
he is not supposed to be here
he is gone   he is gone?

When I wake up this last time
sun peeks in through the window
Yahaira is entwined alongside me

I can feel her heart against my back
I am sweating   & I want to pull away,
I want to bury in the safety.

From the kitchen, I hear Tía's soft steps slow
even from over there she knows I am awake.
I clear my eyes one more time

because I can't tell if there's a figure
in the corner or if it is just a wet pile of clothes
but when I squint I see

Yahaira's mother dozing in a chair.

———————

Fifty-Five Days After

The next morning I find Mami at the little table
in front of the Saints drinking coffee.

I do not sit down before I speak.

"She needs to come back with us. Not because
it's what Papi wanted, but because it's what she most needs.

What we most need." Mami keeps her eyes straight ahead.
Her finger rubbing the smooth rim of the cup.

Mami doesn't say anything in response.
She finishes her coffee, stands up.

She grabs her purse & drives out.
There was so much I had left to say:

That maybe a bad husband can still be a good parent.
That maybe he tried to be the best he knew how to be.

That he hurt her   got caught up   there's no excuse.
But he is not here. He is not here. We are all that's left.

Camino stumbles out of her bedroom looking like
she's been run over by a train.

I know that Camino's pride is like ironing starch
& she sprinkles it over herself until it stiffens her spine.

She didn't tell anyone about the tuition bills.
She didn't tell anyone about the man stalking her.

This whole time she's swallowed her words like bitter pills
not realizing they were slow-drip poison.

I do not know what is going to happen next.
But I cannot   will not   leave without her.

———

Yahaira's mother
comes back to the house
after midday.

& for some reason,
I am waiting for a lecture
on how I acted irresponsibly:

how I stole from her daughter,
how I need to return her money,
how I am no fit sister to her child.

I almost hope she does say
any of those things
so I can loose all the angry things

I hope to say back.
But Yahaira's mother does not say anything.
She sits in the rocking chair next to mine

& our squeaking chairs
hold their own conversation.
I peek at her from the corner of my eyes.

She is a beautiful lady,
but the skin beneath her eyes
is smudged with exhaustion.

As if she feels my gaze on hers she speaks:

"You needed a mother,
& I wasn't sure
I could be that to you.

Your mother & I were friends, you know,
we were good, good friends once.
I thought I would look at you

& see her betrayal on your skin.
See your father's faithlessness in your eye.
I did it to protect myself.

I was so softhearted
when it came to your father.
I didn't want the sight of you to undo me."

Yahaira's mother takes out a folder from her purse.

She passes it to me.
I scan the sheet quickly.
It's an emergency appointment for a visa

scheduled for three days' time.
I look up; the questions must be
shining from my eyes.

"With us, you'll come with us.
You cannot stay here.
That man will come back.

Angrier, as they always do.
It is not safe. Your Tía agrees.
& it is what your father wanted.

The interview was scheduled
for late August anyway. I went
to speak with my cousin to ensure they could push it up."

What I wanted. What I wanted.
For so long. How bittersweet
a realized dream   can be flavored.

———

Does anyone ever
want to leave their home?
The fresh fruit that drops from their backyard?

The neighbors who wiped their snot?
Does anyone ever
want to believe they won't come back?

To the dog that sniffs their heel,
to the bed that holds the echo of their body?
Is there relief in pretending it is temporary,

that one day it will be safe? That I will once again
wave to the kind school bus driver;
that I'll hold Carline's baby before he grows,

having never known me? They have no palm
trees in New York City, no leaves to shade me,
to brush against my cheeks like my mother's hands.

There is no one over there, alive or buried,
who held me as a child, who cradled me close,
who fed me from their table, who wiped my knees when

I fell & scraped them. Here, despite the bad & ugly,
is my home. & now I wish that I could stay. Does anyone ever
want to leave the place they love?

———

While Yahaira & her mother run errands,
I join Tía on a round of the neighborhood.
I haven't seen El Cero in days, but both

Tía & I keep our heads on a swivel.
The last house we visit is the house
of the old woman with cancer.

I pet Vira Lata & order him to wait outside.
I am nervous of what we'll find behind the door.
But when Tía knocks, I see she also pulls a key out.

I look at her with a question in my eyes.
"One of the neighborhood boys installed a lock;
he gave a group of us copies so we could get in & out.

It's safer for her that way." Inside I see
the sheets have been changed recently,
& a vase near the window holds field flowers.

I put my hand on the woman's brow
& she turns her head into my hand.
When I press my fingers to her stomach

the lump there seems to have grown smaller.
I shake my head at Tía; none of this makes sense.
She squeezes my hand.

———◆———

Carline comes over that night.
She brings a small wrapped box
& wishes me a happy belated birthday.

I hold her tightly before I introduce her
to Yahaira's mother; she had not met her at the funeral.
Carline must be surprised by the woman but does not let on.

She tells me Luciano has been breathing better,
& he even cried for the first time. His lungs:
clearer, stronger. I have hope he will live.

We do not say the word *milagro*,
but I know that like a flame,
Tía wrought a miracle & Carline nurtured it.

I squeeze her hand
& an idea spins in my head.
Tía refuses to leave here. She says she is needed.

But she is going to require help when I'm gone,
& she needs new blood to teach.
Carline's house is packed to the brim with people

but here is a house that will sit mostly empty,
& an apprenticeship that she would be perfect for.
Having Nelson around the house would be helpful,

& Tía loves little more than a baby to cradle,
a family to feed.
I will broach the idea with Tía tomorrow,

the Saints in my ears whisper, sí mi'ja, sí mi'ja, sí.

———

Yahaira's mother takes me
to the clinic to get a health report;
the civil registry office

to obtain a copy of my birth certificate,
to make a copy of her marriage record
that shows she is legally my stepmother.

We spend hours in the rental car
driving from here to there & back,
Yahaira sleeping in at home or helping Tía.

Zoila & I speak little on these trips,
but when I'm humming along to a song,
she turns up the radio.

& when her face was red from heat
in the clinic waiting room,
I used a magazine to fan it.

It is awkward, these familial ties   & breaks we share.
But we are muddling through it. With Yahaira
brokering our silence when she can. & by letting the hurt

between us soothe itself quiet when she can't.

———◆———

I dress nicely for the consular agency in Puerto Plata.
I tug on my graduation dress, that was my priest meeting dress,
that is now my visa interview dress. I am clothed

in beginnings & endings. A lucky & unlucky garment.
But isn't every life adorned with both?
We will see what this black brings me today.

Zoila sits in the interview room with me
as her cousin asks me questions.
When he asks about school, I tell him I want to study premed
    at Columbia.

The consular officer tells us
it will take a couple of days to process,
but he shakes my hand warmly & gives Zoila a wink.

———◆———

My mother & Camino leave the house
every day preparing for her visa appointment.

I let them spend the hours without me.
I do not want to be a crutch for either of them to use to hobble.

Instead, I spend time in Tía's garden,
& think of Dre with her tomato plants.

Twice Carline has come over, once with the baby,
strapped to her chest.

He is a small boy, & when I stroked his cheek
he opened his eyelids & stared at me.

This made Carline gasp. She told me the baby is five weeks old,
& she's been scared this whole time he would not make it.

But his steady gaze on mine makes me believe
this babe was born a warrior & he isn't going anywhere.

One morning, after Mami & Camino climbed into the Prius,
I walked down to her beachfront. Glancing sideways to make
     sure

I was not being followed, although I felt like I was being watched,
I stood at the water's edge. I could imagine my father here.

This wide world of trees, & rocks, & water:
a kingdom he presided over. I could imagine him a boy,

in chancletas & a small T-shirt running here to dive,
& climb trees, & imagine a great big world.

I skim my feet in the water, with my face stroked by the sun
& pretend it is my father   hands on my skin

saying sorry   I love you   welcome home   goodbye.
I forgive you.   I forgive you.   I forgive you.

Say the waves.   Say I.

——◆——

The night after the consular visit,
Yahaira tells me she has someone she wants me to meet.
& since she can't possibly know anyone in this callejón that I
    don't,

I know she means in the United States.
"I'm excited to meet your friends when I get there,"
I say politely. Ever since the night with El Cero

it's been more difficult to be snarky with her.

She shakes her head.
"I want you to meet her before we arrive,
& she wants to meet you too. My girlfriend, Dre."

She says this firmly. Looking me in the eye.
& I know what she thinks. I will condemn her
for being gay. Homosexuality is complicated here.

I look at her right back. "We should video-chat with her."
& she pulls out her phone, presses a name
from the speed-dial screen.

Soon, a dark-skinned girl with short hair fills the screen.
She smiles with all her teeth when she sees Yahaira.
"Hey, baby! Two calls in one day! Lucky me."

Yahaira turns the phone a bit so the girl & I are face-to-face.
I pull back in surprise. Not because of this girl, Dre.
But because it's the first time I've seen our faces like this,

side by side, almost pressed against each other.
I clear my throat, suddenly nervous; this is someone
my sister loves. If she does not love me my sister might not
   either.

"Hello, Dre," I say; my English sounds a bit rusty.
Dre answers back, & asks me how I'm doing
in excellent Spanish. Thank God she speaks it.

Then she surprises me completely by changing locations.
I follow her via the screen as she walks into a bedroom,
then pulls away a grate that covers a window.

Yahaira whispers to me, "She wants to show you something
on the fire escape. She loves to grow things."
When the body holding the phone heaves through the window,

I hear the loudness of honking cars & people yelling.
The screen flips so I see a planter against a railing,
then the little green buds aiming toward the sky.

Dre's face again fills the screen. "Yahaira told me your
aunty is a healer & that sometimes you help. I thought
starting you a little herb garden might help make you feel more
    at home."

Moisture stings my eyes & I nod at Dre.
Then lean over to Yahaira, fake whispering in English,
"Where did you find her?

& is there a clone of her somewhere that I could marry?"

———•———

Fifty-Nine Days After

The night before we leave DR
we sit around the table,

the four of us
eating toasted cassava & butter.

Vira Lata sits at Tía's heel,
the way he has since the night at the beach.

Mami says she thinks it would be good
if when we get back home

we return to the counseling sessions.
& I know it has scared her

how big the emotions
of loss have weighed on our shoulders.

Enough for me to disobey her
in a way I never have.

Enough for her to forget
the kind of woman she once was.

Enough for Camino
to thrust herself into unleashed danger.

Tía does not say much,
but she cleans crumbs

from the corner of Camino's mouth
& she butters a piece of cassava

that she passes to me
like she has hand-fed me my whole life.

———————

Sixty Days After

At the airport
Tía does not cry.
But I cannot *stop* crying.

I am a small child again
an ocean   a big loss of stream.
But Tía, as Tía has always been,

is mountainous in her small stature.
& it's all I need:
for her to be an immovable rock,

to know she will still be here
when I decide to come back.
Before I turn from her

she touches the string of beads
between her breasts & then taps her fingers
to my own heart.

The pulse of her heart
matching my own; a rhythm
neither time nor oceans can make offbeat.

& I know she is saying she is with me

& so are the Saints.
She stands in the terminal
until I walk through security.

Gives me a nod.
& I see her mouth:
"Que Dios te bendiga, mi'ja."

I stop moving. How can I leave her?
She seems so small   alone.
She is my home. I already miss her.

She shakes her head,
as if she can read my thoughts,
she shoos me with her hands.

Onward. Always onward.

I blow her a kiss
across the linoleum, &
whisper blessings under my breath,

divide a piece of God
from my heart
for her to carry.

I know she does the same for me.

As the plane from DR
begins down the runway

I reach for Camino's hand.
She has her head pushed

into the backrest, her eyes clenched,
mouthing prayers.

But our fingers intertwine
& don't let go until
the pilot hops on the loudspeaker.

He assures us the flight path is clear.

Tells us to enjoy the beverage service.
My heart stops beating quite so hard.

Camino opens her eyes,
staring at the water

       endless & blue beneath us.

I tell her that when we land
some people on the plane might clap.

She turns to me with an eyebrow raised.
I imagine it's kind of giving thanks.
Of all the ways it could end

it ends not with us in the sky or the water,

but together
    on solid earth
        safely grounded.

———

AUTHOR'S NOTE

MY FIRST MEMORY OF VISITING THE DOMINICAN REPUBLIC IS ALSO my first memory of being on a flight. I was taken to visit my mother's family, many of whom I had met only once when I was six months old, and none of whom now, at eight years old, I had any memories of. I was escorted on my flight by a neighbor, Doña Reina, and while I was excited, I was also so nervous, having no family I was familiar with nearby. My mother dressed me formally: a scratchy tweedlike dress and a big hat with a sunflower around the brim. This was a big deal. The flight itself scared me: Why were we in the air so long? If I slept, would they forget to collect me from the plane? What would happen if the whole thing fell?

My favorite moment was when the plane landed and the other passengers clapped. Instinctively I joined them. Even if the exact performance we were applauding was unclear, it was understood; it was praise for a higher being for allowing us to arrive safely, as a reaction to the pilot's performance, applause for ourselves at having finally returned—I didn't know then, and I don't know now, the exact reason for that spontaneous reaction, but I know I was enamored with the many ways Dominicans celebrate touching down onto our island.

When I was thirteen years old, two months and one day after September 11, 2001, flight AA587 crashed to the ground in Queens, New York. It was on its way to Santo Domingo, Dominican Republic. Two hundred sixty people, plus five people on the ground, died. More than 90 percent of the passengers were of Dominican descent. Many were returning home. It completely rocked the New York Dominican community. It is the second-deadliest aviation crash in United States history.

There was so much confusion around the November crash; I remember the special mass held at church, the bewilderment my father expressed as he read Dominican newspapers for more information, the candlelight vigils held outside the apartment buildings where passengers on that flight had lived. I also remember how little this crash was remembered when it was determined the cause was not terrorism. How quickly the news coverage trickled off, how it seemed the larger societal memory had moved on, even though the collective memory of my community was still wrestling with the loss.

Throughout the years, I've circled back to the details of that flight. Knowing I wanted to remember. Knowing I wanted a larger narrative that commemorated that moment in time. My research led me to so many stories of individuals who were returning to the Dominican Republic to retire, to open grocery stores, to help a sick relative, or to celebrate their military leave. My research also led me to stories of people with multiple families, with large secrets, with truths that were exposed publicly and without pomp after their death.

Most families are messy; most parents will fail to live up to the hero worship of their children. In *Clap When You Land*, I wanted to write a story that considered who matters and deserves attention in the media, as well as a more intimate portrayal of what it means to discover secrets, to discover family, to discover the depths of your own character in the face of great loss—and gain.

ACKNOWLEDGMENTS

I want to give thanks to my editor, Rosemary Brosnan, and my fantastic team at HarperTeen, including, but not limited to: Courtney Stevenson, Erin Fitzsimmons, Sari Murray, Shona McCarthy, and Ebony LaDelle. Thanks for helping me tell stories that deal in tenderness and immense love of my community.

I want to give thanks to Joan Paquette for believing in this book, and to Alexandra Machinist for her thoughtful guidance.

I had fantastic beta readers who showed this story so much early love that I felt brave enough to tell it. Thanks to my bestie, Carid Santos, a million times over. She sat with this story through so many drafts and continuously gave an example for the sisterhood I wanted to forge here. Special thanks to readers Yahaira Castro, Safia Elhillo, Clint Smith, Daniel José Older, Phil Bildner, and Limer Batista. Camino and Yahaira are truer because of your keen eyes and big hearts and kinship. And shout-out to Ibi Zoboi, who listened to my idea about this story when it had only one main character and said, in no uncertain terms: you need to voice the other sister.

I had two mothers who helped midwife this story. Thanks to my momma, Rosa, who answered all my questions about Hora Santas, and holistic healing, and comadronas, and curanderas, and prayed—literally prayed—when I told her I was stuck: the answer to writer's block, in my case, seems to be my mother's supreme faith. And special thanks to my mother-in-law, Ms. Sarah Cannon-Moye, who talked me through so many sticky points when I was ready to throw my laptop out the window. Her patience and belief in me, as well as her tough questions, were critical to my undoing the knots in the narrative.

Thank you to my family, the Amadis and Acevedos, the Paulinos and Minayas. Thank you for welcoming me in Santo Domingo and letting me be one of your own. Special thanks to the Batistas—meeting you all at eight years old felt like finding sisters.

Shakir Amman Cannon-Moye: you're my favorite. Thank you for standing beside me through both the applause and the crash landings.

Ancestors, as always, I write to you / for you / with you, carrying the utmost love and reverence. Thank you for wedging open so many doorways that have led to my wildest dreams; I promise to continue walking through them.